I0545350

Kit Kringle:
An Alaskan Tale

Dani Haviland

USA Today Bestselling Author

Kit Kringle: An Alaskan Tale is a work of fiction.

Names, places, characters, and incidents are either the product of the author's imagination or are used fictitiously for the reader's entertainment.

Any resemblance to persons, living, dead or fictional; events or locales is entirely coincidental.

Copyright 2017

Dani Haviland

Chill Out! Books

ISBN: 978-1-946752-15-4

Chapter 1
Anchorage, Alaska
Late November

Kay walked in the front door and saw the young, scruffy mechanic sitting at the desk. "Hi, there, Jay! Do you guys need any parts or supplies today?"

"Well, good morning. Um, yes," he said, rubbing a hand across his stubble-whiskered chin, trying to think of what he could possibly order from her so she'd have to come back. "I'd like about twenty to thirty 3/8-inch fine thread hard bolts, nuts, lock washers, and flats, please."

"So, do you want twenty or thirty? And don't you have those in your bolt bins? I mean, I'm sure your boss would rather you use those than spend money with me."

Jay chuckled and shook his head. "I really don't care what he wants. He's going to charge his customer double what you charge us for parts anyhow. He can use his reclaimed hardware on something he rebuilds. I want to use all new parts if that's what he's charging the customer for. He may be the one doing the billing, but I'm the mechanic who signs off on it. I haven't done much in this town, so don't have a reputation. Yet. When word gets around that I get it done right the first time, I won't have to be begging for jobs or working for a guy like Lumpy. Oh, and go ahead and get me thirty sets. I don't want you running back and forth to get a few at a time from the hardware store. I'm sure I'll be needing more of them somewhere else later."

"Okay. Are you up to snuff with anti-seize, shop rags, floor dry, hand cleaner..." Kay asked and bent over her notepad, ready to add to her meager list.

"Now that you mention it, all of the above. Lumpy just got paid for cleaning up some old guy's yard. I guess there was enough scrap copper there for salvage that he'll be able to make this month's rent, fill his truck with fuel, and still have some set aside for parts." Jay shook his head. "And, most likely, another bender. When will he ever learn?"

Kay shrugged her shoulder as she finished penciling in the remainder of her shopping list. She should be able to get the goods in two stops, not three. Cool, the stores were next door to each other, too, so not much gas needed. "As my daddy used to say to the guys who worked for him, 'Integrity is like virginity: once you've lost it, you can never get it back."

Jay laughed so hard, he nearly spat out his coffee. "Sorry about that," he said and wiped the dribble from his chin. "We have another Cat coming in tomorrow as soon as the sun comes up, probably about 10 or so. I'll have a big parts order for you shortly thereafter. I have a preliminary list going but won't know the extent of the damages to the final drive until after I pull the covers. Until then," he lifted his thermal coffee mug in salute and said dryly, "Have a nice day." He grabbed the door handle to let her out, then added a charismatic grin that made Kay suppress an automatic wiggle in reply. "I mean it. I'll see you tomorrow."

"Um, uh," Kay stuttered, undone by his sly smile, "Didn't you want the hardware and other goodies before that?"

"Oh, yeah. Go ahead and bring them over when you get a chance. I'll be here."

Still undone by his flirtatious and suggestive manner, Kay didn't even try to speak. Instead she kept her head down as she headed to her car and issued a generic 'farewell, I'll get the heck out of here, I'm sure you're busy' wave.

As soon as she got in her car, Kay let out a huge sigh of released tension. Yes, he was cute. He didn't speak much, and she didn't know much about him other than he had been in trouble with the law at some point, that he had met Lumpy while they were both in jail, and that he was much younger than she was. And that he was apparently flirting with her now.

Or was she flirting with him?

Nah. She couldn't afford the emotional energy to flirt. And even if she could, she wouldn't allow herself the luxury. She had a business to get established and romantic entanglements, even brief ones, were not on the agenda. Not many women had the gumption to start a business at 40 years old, much less taking on the construction industry in the logistical nightmare of Alaska. What had she been thinking? And why here?

Well, that was the easiest question she'd asked herself all day. She started it in Alaska because that's where she was when it was either compromise her virtue, starve, or go home to Missouri and live with Mama after the romance that brought her north fizzled out.

The application for the business license was simple enough and there weren't any sales taxes to bother with. Buy parts on credit cards, sell them at a mark up, get paid by the customer right away, take enough money for food, rent, and gas, then pay what was left over to the credit card companies. Simple enough, right?

However, she hadn't counted on the bias. 'Alaska: Where men were men and women won the Iditarod,' didn't apply to the prejudice she had encountered in the last year as she tried to get established as a reliable vendor. Too many of the wholesalers she had encountered had wanted more than her business. "Let's talk about it over dinner or drinks," usually meant let's go out drinking and if you'll put out, I'll give you Net 30 credit. She was glad she hadn't fallen for that one even once, although she did have to slap a few hands first. You'd think that these men, some of them married, had never seen a woman before and thought that they should be allowed to touch her just because she was female.

Shoot. She knew more about tractors and heavy equipment then most men her age. Her father had taught her well. Growing up on construction sites was the best education she could have earned. If she had been a male instead of a female, no one would have thought twice about trusting her as a parts supplier. "Yes," she said softly to herself as she started her little Chevy Sonic, "Alaska: the odds are good, but the goods are odd. I sure hope it was a woman who put that on tee shirts and that she made enough money from it that she didn't need to depend on a man."

Kay pulled out of the parking lot. "Quit thinking about men, Kay. Get downtown, pick up those supplies for Jay, make sure you get paid by Lumpy before he drinks up what money he has left, then get back to calling on more contractors. There has to be a way to make money in this state without a college degree or driving a truck." She sped up to get on the highway. "Or without being on your back or knees."

Chapter 2

The cat crouched in the snow flattened by tire tracks, waiting for its chance to pounce on the magpie. A car turned into the parking lot and scared the bird away. The cat followed it, leaping over snow berms and broken branches in a desperate attempt to make it dinner.

Kay tried opening the door to the shop, but it was locked. She knocked on it, then realized that her gloves muffled the noise. "Dang, it's cold today," she said as she pulled one glove off and rapped with her bare knuckles.

Still no reply. The whir of the impact gun starting and stopping meant that someone was getting busy in there. She put her glove back on and pounded on the door with the side of her fist.

Still no reply, but now the noises also included the loud clanging of metal on concrete.

Kay dropped her bundles to the side of the door, went back to her little red car, and grabbed her snow removal tool. No use bruising her hands. *Smack, smack, smack!*

Clink, clank, clunk. The unmistakable sound of a wrench hitting the floor, then other bits and pieces of metal dropping preceded the shuffle of boots and a quick tug on the door. "What are you doing out here. It's freezing and..." Jay reached around and twisted the door knob from the outside. "Oops. I forgot to unlock it. Here, let me carry this stuff in. Did you get everything?"

Kay hurried past Jay as he bent to load up the shop supplies she had dropped. "I have the hardware. You got the rest there. Now, all I have to do is find Lumpy to give him his invoice. You know, he makes such a big deal about getting paid right away, but when it comes time to pay his own bills, he has more excuses than a grizzly bear has hair follicles."

"That's Lumpy, all right."

Kay handed him the hardware. "Why *do* they call him Lumpy, anyway? He's not fat."

Jay took the box and picked through the pieces, putting the washers on a bolt, then adding the nut, busying himself to keep her around longer. "His real name is Larry, but he's always telling anyone who'll listen that he's had more than his fair share of lumps in life, so folks started calling him Lumpy."

Kay wasn't in any hurry to go back into the cold, so stood under the unit heater and made small talk. "By the way, I saw that cat or lynx or whatever it is run across the parking lot towards the back yard again. I think I'll put some food out for it and see what happens."

"I already did last week," Jay said, continuing to assemble all the bolts, washers, and nuts in the box.

"Did it eat the food?"

"Either it did or the ravens did. I didn't see any droppings, though. Naw, I think the cat got to it first."

"So, it's a cat, not a lynx?" Kay asked, pulling off her gloves so her fingers could thaw out in the blast of heated forced air.

"I don't know. Can't get close enough to tell, but even if it is a lynx, it's still a cat."

"I think I'll call it Yardley."

"Why?"

"Because either she or he lives in the yard. But I think it's a she because she's been flirting with you for the last week."

"She's not flirting with me; she's cozying up to the food. I could be an automatic-feeder and she'd love me just as much. But you're right. A guy cat would chase his food down rather than accept a handout. Females want to have their dinner brought right to them."

"Bullshit."

"What? I didn't think you cussed."

"Only when riled. You think that I don't chase down every dollar I make? Do you see any man around me paying my bills? Do you, do you… Ergh! I work hard for what I earn. It doesn't make a difference whether I'm a man or a woman, either. And just for the record, I didn't ask to be born female. I am what I am and gender has nothing to do with the fact that I'd rather be self-employed than laze around all winter, collecting unemployment or welfare, or living off of someone else, or starving."

"Sorry. I didn't mean to make you mad…"

"Well, you did. And I know plenty of lazy men who even though they 'have a job,' are worthless and don't work a lick. They may have a time card to fill out, but that doesn't mean they earn that paycheck. And I can name three men right off the top of my head who are letting their girlfriends or wives support them over the winter while they wait for hunting or fishing season to open."

"Okay, okay. I get it. It's the person, not the gender. I

guess I've just been around the wrong type of woman most of my life."

"Well, look around. I'm not that type."

Jay inhaled deeply, ready to tell her he had already noticed, then bit the side of his cheek to keep from commenting.

"Give this to Lumpy for me if and when you see him. I gotta go."

Jay held the door open for her, "See ya," he said, hoping it would be soon. And for more than just two minutes.

Chapter 3

The next evening

Kay turned the knob. It was unlocked. It was past six, but there were still mechanical noises in the shop. Either Jay had decided to dig deeper into that dozer final drive or Lumpy had decided to help his one and only employee. The tall gray-haired man repeatedly told her what a great mechanic he was, but she had never seen him touch a wrench, much less use one.

"Anyone here?" she asked to let her presence be known.

"Hey, there! How's the prettiest little parts gal in the whole state of Alaska doing tonight?" Lumpy asked, wiping the fried chicken bits from his mouth. "No, wait. I'm doing you an injustice. The prettiest little parts gal in the whole USA."

Kay looked over at Jay who was walking out from behind the disabled bulldozer, wiping down the combination wrench with one of the new shop cloths she had sold him. He rolled his eyes at her and shook his head in disgust. 'Such a womanizer,' he said without uttering a word.

"Me? I'm doing fine. I baked some banana nut bread and

thought I'd share it with you two, being bachelors and all. Besides, I had some bananas that were past prime for my corn flakes and I wanted to heat up the apartment a little more. Oh, and Jay, did you ever finish that parts list? I can get working on it right away. If I place the order online tonight, they can ship out tomorrow. Even if I got the list from you at 8:00 a.m. sharp, I'd miss the shipping cut off for the day. Those four hours of time difference between here and the east coast sure play havoc at times."

"I got it over here. Just get me prices on these starred items. If they cost too much, I'll weld them up and reuse them. If they're cheap enough, it would cost the owner more in my time than the part." Jay finished his comment, then looked across the room at Lumpy.

Kay followed his eyes and saw that Lumpy had taken one of the three mini loaves and was eating it like a donut, wolfing it down, his cheeks crammed full. Lumpy looked back at Jay. "I figured I'd leave one of these for you. Or maybe not. These are great. Thanks, Kay."

"Um, you're welcome. And if you don't mind, I'd like to get paid for the invoice I left for you yesterday. I have some bills to pay and some of the stuff I picked up I had to pay for out of pocket. Not everyone gives me Net 30 days."

"You gave me a bill? I never got one. Jay, did this sweet young lady hand you an invoice and you didn't give it to me?"

Jay clenched his jaws in frustration. Lumpy was a liar—he and everyone who knew the man was aware of that—but to blame him for something he didn't do was despicable. He walked over to the work bench and the paper plate loaded with chicken bones and lifted up the can of cola. "It's right here, under your pop. You said you'd get to it later. Well, it's later."

Kay wasn't sure what to do, but she knew she needed that money. Ugh, time to grovel for what was hers. "Lumpy, I'd really appreciate it if you could take care of this tonight."

Hmph! The disgruntled boss had been caught in a lie, but he was Teflon and wasn't about to let it stick. "Sorry about that, gal. I was just needing to get some change." He pulled out a roll of cash and peeled off two one-hundred dollar bills. "I need to pay some bills, too, and I don't have the change."

Jay reached in his pocket, pulled out a thin packet of folded over cash, and pulled out two five-dollar bills. "There's your change. I'm sure Kay will pay me back when she gets the chance. She's one of those folks whose word means something." He grabbed his Carhart coat off the peg, looked over at the plate with the two remaining banana nut loaves on it, took one, and said, "Thanks for supper, Kay. Next time, it's my treat," and walked out the door.

"You know he likes you, don't you? He likes you a lot," Lumpy said, as he picked bread crumbs off the front of his shirt, sticking them in his mouth.

"I know he likes me. I mean, he's not ornery and doesn't blow smoke in my face like some of the guys I call on, but no. He doesn't like me a lot. You said he has a girlfriend and besides the fact that I don't want any romantic entanglements, he's a lot younger than I am. Shoot, he's a baby."

Lumpy snorted at the remark. "Oh, he's no baby, but I guess someone my age is better suited for you. I mean, I'm just a few years older, and wiser, and have a few more years of sexual experience…"

"Oh, my," Kay said as she looked down at her watch, not even noticing the time. "I better get back to my place and fire up the computer. I have some research to do to find you the best prices. Jay said that the customer wants to get these parts right away, not to worry about the cost, that the dozer needed to get back to work at the snow dump right away."

"That's my gal. Don't worry about the cost. Stick with me, and I'll have you living the high life in no time."

"G'night. I'll be in touch," Kay said, and hurried out the door.

It had started snowing in the short time she was inside. "Welcome to Alaska," she said softly as she brushed the snow off her windshield. "I should have known it was going to snow when I saw the temperature rising."

It wasn't the first time Lumpy had made a half-hearted pass at her, but she hoped it would be the last. She hated that she needed him as a customer, but the bigger companies just weren't ready to invest in a small—rather, a micro—company, no matter how able and well-performing it was. Word of mouth was just starting, but it was winter. The only companies that used heavy equipment were dealing with snow removal. And, no matter how tough things got, she did *not* want to sell truck parts. That was a whole different arena, and one that she wasn't comfortable in.

"Stick with me, and I'll have you living the high life in no time," she aped in Lumpy's southern accent. "Yeah, if 'the high life' means living in a mezzanine above your heavy equipment shop, taking baths in the shop sink, eating whatever you can nuke in a microwave or scarfing down fast food." She shuddered in disgust, then cranked the defroster fan up to full power. "Take me home, little red Sonic."

It was ten o'clock by the time she had finished sourcing the parts for Jay's tractor. She caught herself sighing at the thought. It wasn't his tractor, but he was responsible for it. They hadn't talked much, but she got the idea that Lumpy was just a beginning step for him making his way in the world. He had given Lumpy that ten dollars so he didn't have an excuse for not paying her. True, it could have been that Lumpy's two one-hundred dollar bills were wrapped around a wad of singles, but she was pretty sure Jay didn't have much more than the ten bucks he had shelled out. She'd be at the bank at 10:00 AM sharp, deposit most of the money, and make sure she repaid him right away.

***

Two minutes after her head hit the pillow, she was out. Morning came quickly, but that didn't mean it was daylight. It was early December and the sun wasn't up for another couple of hours. Today, like every day, she was awake at

17

7:15 AM. She didn't even own an alarm clock other than the one on her phone, and she hadn't bothered figuring out how to use that one. Time management was the most important reason she was self-employed: she liked setting her own schedule.

"Call and make sure my orders went through and the parts can ship today, check emails, take a shower, eat breakfast, go to the bank, and then return the money to Jay." A smile crept across her face. "Stop that," she told herself aloud. "Do not smile at the thought of a man, any man, at least for another year or two. When you're totally self-sufficient, have all those confounded credit cards paid off, an apartment bigger than a walk-in closet—or better yet, a real house—then you can ooh and sigh over men all you want.

***

"Would you like to apply for our low introductory fee credit card," the teller asked. "You're already pre-approved because you're a member of this bank."

"No, thank you. Oh, and would you make sure I get at least two five-dollar bills in change?"

"No problem. Have a nice day, ma'am."

When did I go from being a miss to a ma'am? Do I look

that old? What is the cut off age? I thought it was fifty. Shoot, I'm not even forty! Kay caught her reflection in the plate glass window. *Whether you're a miss or a ma'am, you still have your figure. And if what Lumpy says is true, Jay likes you.*

"Oh, shut up," she said aloud, trying to quiet the voices in her head.

"Pardon me?" asked the older woman who had passed her outside the bank.

"Oh, excuse me. I was just talking to myself. Sometimes I have to say something out loud or I won't listen."

The older woman laughed and shook her head. "Honey, I'm glad I'm not the only one. Don't let anyone tell you to hush, either." She leaned down and whispered to Kay, "But you might want to make sure there isn't anyone around when you tell yourself to shut up."

The two of them shared a chuckle then parted ways. *Yes, the other woman was older, but was still attractive. Will that be me in a few years? Will I look worse? Do I want to wait to find a man?*

Kay looked around to make sure she was alone, then got in her car, turned the engine on, and said very loudly, "Shut up. You don't need a man," then left the parking lot, heading to Lumpy's shop.

Chapter 4

Kay watched as the shaggy cat scampered across the road, into the shop parking lot, then disappeared behind the building.

"Hey, there!"

Kay jumped. "Oh, hi, Jay. I didn't see you. Were you in the secret service or something? You're always so quiet."

"No, and I think that would be the CIA or SEALS. The secret service guys are pretty obvious, all dressed up in their suits and dark sunglasses, standing right in front of the president or whoever it is they're protecting."

"Oh, yeah. Right. Hey, I saw our cat just now. Man, she was hightailing it from out front of the shop to the back yard. Do you think she'll survive the winter?"

"Our cat?" Jay said and smiled as if Kay had just revealed her bra size to him.

"I mean, *the* cat. You know, Yardley. He or she sure has a lot of life left for being outside this long. It was ten below last week and I don't think he/she belongs to anyone."

Jay opened the door and let her inside. "Anyone but herself. I got a close look at her when she was eating some of that cat food I left outside on that old D3. If it was a male, he must have froze his balls off."

Kay stifled a laugh with the back of her hand, then changed her mind and let it go. "So, you feed the cat on the Cat?"

"Yup. And she has the thickest, most matted coat I've ever seen. She's a mess, but I guess it keeps the cold out. Her tracks go in and out under that one old orange connex out back. I noticed that there haven't been any voles in the shop, either. They usually come in once it starts freezing. Yup, she's not a lazy female: she goes out and works for her keep, just like someone else I know."

Kay blushed, then wondered why. He was flattering her, but also apologizing for insinuating that women were lazy. Score one for Jay being a good person, regardless of whether he'd seen the inside of a jail cell or not.

"Oh, I just remembered. I have some money for you. Thanks for standing up to Lumpy for me. I really didn't think he was going to give me the money. You sort of forced his hand." She handed him the two five-dollar bills. "And the next time I bake, I'll make sure I give you yours before I give him any. That is, if I do decide to share with him. He doesn't seem too generous or even helpful. Does he even work on any of these tractors?"

"Nope. He'll pop his head over my shoulder every once in a while, tell me I'm doing something wrong, then walk away. He just wants to feel like he's in charge. Well, he is, in a way. He does manage to get a customer or two talked into letting him repair trucks or tractors, but he doesn't do the work. He gets some down on his luck guy like me in here to pull the wrenches, then he takes all the credit. And cash. He hasn't stiffed me yet, but he knows not to cross me."

Kays eyes widened. Maybe she had a warm spot for the wrong guy. Was he violent?

Jay laughed when he saw her discomfort. "No, I'm not a tough guy. And I can probably count the times I've yelled at someone on one hand. People are afraid of me because I'm quiet and because I'm big. The chatty kinds or the runts are the ones who get run over."

"Um, I didn't think you were that tall," Kay said, then grimaced.

Jay walked over to her without saying a word, stopped

just inches from her, then straightened up. He saw her back away in fear.

"See what I mean about being quiet and tall? It scares people. I just use it when needed. I would never hurt you. And woe be to anyone who tries to mess with you. Lumpy hasn't laid a hand on you, has he?"

"No, but he sure makes suggestions. Not direct ones, he just crows about his sexual prowess and big feet. Then he tries to get me interested in him by telling me how much money he usually has, but that he's just in a dry spell right now."

"Feet lie, and he's a chronic liar. I've known him for a year and a half now, and every time he gets money, he drinks it away. That's why I make sure that my rent is part of my wages and that he pays me every Friday for the cash portion."

"Oh. I never thought about where you lived. I mean..." Kay's face reddened. "Excuse me," she said as she fanned herself with her little notebook. "I didn't think I was old enough, but I think I'm having hot flashes."

Phew! Dodged that one for now. Maybe she could use that excuse for another year or two. 'I'm old enough to be going through menopause' should scare off any man. And what was that about feet? She looked over at the floor where Jay was and saw him lifting his boot to show that he didn't have big feet. Shit.

"By the way, I got good news," Kay said in a strained effort to recuperate. "All your parts should be in tomorrow."

Jay answered her with a sly grin, "And I have good news for you, too. I may be pissing him off, but I really don't care. I took the price you were quoting Lumpy, doubled it, and told the owner of this Cat that he was to pay you direct. It's a big chunk of change and I know you'll get it right away. All you need to do is go downtown to his office with an invoice and his secretary will cut you a check while you wait. This nonsense of not paying you when I know that wad really was all hundreds, is for the birds. On a parts sale this big, he'd have it blown before the bars closed."

"Are you sure Lumpy won't get mad and fire you or get back at you some other way?"

"He can't get too mad because it's my customer. I got the deal, not him. When I hired on, he told me I could work on my own stuff in his shop if he didn't have something else in it. Well, he didn't have anything else, not even any

25

prospects. He's out chasing some gold miner right now. Something about they need a big generator. He has an old Detroit he's been trying to get rid of ever since I met him, but this guy wants Caterpillar only, so I think he's screwed."

"Really," Kay drawled. "I just happen to have a father who has a friend who refurbishes and sells old Cat generators. I don't want to take away his customer. I mean, that wouldn't be very ladylike, much less civilized, so I may have a word with Mr. Lumpy. Maybe I can upgrade to a one-bedroom apartment from my studio by Christmas if this plays out..."

"Be careful when working with Lumpy. Just a minute ago, you were seeing right through him. Right now, you have that dollar sign blindness going on. Don't do anything I wouldn't do."

"Well, since I don't know much about you, I can't say whether I will or won't, but I will be careful."

Jay watched as she walked out the door. She was smart, determined, and cute, and that round bottom of hers was worth a second look any and every time. Now, as long as she didn't do something stupid like fall under that snake charmer's wiles, maybe he'd get to know her better. Her and that perky hot-flashing figure, a lot better.

***

"You give me the specs your customer needs and I'll see if I can get him what he wants."

"Now you're talking, young lady," Lumpy said, cautiously placing his arm around her.

Kay cleared her throat, and slinked down and away from his test move. She knew if she let him get away with a casual touch, she'd be fighting off the old fart fist, tooth, and nail before the month was out. She wanted the sale, but nothing was worth getting 'friendly' with him.

"As I was saying, I can get Cat generators. I don't want to go around you, so I'll sell it to you, then you sell it to him. I do need to get paid up front, though. I can't carry $1,000 much less $40,000."

"You stick with me, young lady, and you'll be keeping a thousand dollars cash in that little change purse of yours. Here, I have a copy of what's needed by my gold miner buddy up near Fairbanks. You get a 350KW generator quoted to the Port of Anchorage, and I'll take care of it from there. You see, I have this trucker friend who owes me. I'll get him to take it up to Nenana, and the customer can drag it

27

in to his mine from there with a D8. I'll set the price to him, then we'll split the profit, 50-50."

Kay looked down at the photocopied spec sheet. It looked like this request had been making the used equipment circuit for quite a while. Carl's name had been crossed off as had Sully's. Either Lumpy was being careless and had given her the wrong copy or he thought she was stupid. It was better for her if it was the latter. It was easier to watch a man hiding aces up his sleeve if he thought no one was looking.

"I'll get back to you tomorrow afternoon. Everyone has closed down for the day back east and even if I do get in touch with the right person, he always needs to make sure someone else doesn't have a sale pending."

"What? I thought you were going to take care of this right away, little lady. Are you slipping?" Lumpy asked, his hand reaching out to stroke her arm.

"No, I'm not slipping," Kay said and moved further away. "And you've had this information for how long and are just now sharing it with me?" she asked, glaring at him, hoping he'd squirm for making light of her skills.

"Oh, don't worry about it. I knew you could find something quick as a Playboy bunny," he replied, once again trying to wrap an arm around her, this time for a full-blown hug.

Kay backed further away, stifling the urge to slap him. "Would you be acting like this if I was a man? Would you try groping or hugging Jay or any other person you work with?"

"Of course not. They're not my type. I mean, I'm not queer or nothing. You're a fine woman and you need a man to take care of you. I'll help you all that I can, but you need to give me something in return. You know what I mean?" he said with a wink, then licked his lips.

"I'll do just fine by myself," Kay said. "I'll get back to you tomorrow about that generator. By phone." She turned to leave, then looked back. "And have a good night."

As soon as she was out of the parking lot, she let loose. "Ergh! Son of a bitchin' whore monger, shit-eating, cock-su… No, wait, he said he didn't do that. Asshole! I do *not* need a man!"

As was her habit in the winter, she started braking way before the stop sign, and was glad she had. The four-way stop was polished ice for at least fifty feet before the signs in every direction, the street lights reflecting off the uneven mirrored surface, giving the area an eerie glow. Her brakes shuddered as the ABS automatic skid control kicked in. She came to a complete stop, looked all three ways, then saw the one-ton pickup truck barreling toward the intersection on her right. There was no way he'd be able to stop, so she braced herself and waited, hoping he'd get it under control at the last moment.

No such luck. The driver slid up to the intersection, fishtailing then spinning like an Olympic ice skater. He finally came to a halt when the passenger side of his truck smacked hers, her two-year old vehicle taking the full brunt of the impact, before his rebounded.

"Shit! Shit! Shit!" she screamed as she pounded the horn in frustration.

Suddenly, the driver of the truck was at her window, pounding on it with gloved hand, urging her to roll it down. "Are you all right?" he asked.

"Hell no! You just wrecked my car. And it's only two years old. And I have a $500 deductible on it. You are insured, aren't you? Hey, I want to see your insurance papers right now."

The middle-aged man with the black knit cap pulled low over his head blocked her from getting out with his leg held close to the door. "Hold on," he said, and pulled off his glove with his teeth.

"I want to get out," Kay said, and tried again to open the door.

"Stay put," the man said gruffly. "I want to make this right, but if I get any more points on my license, they'll throw me in jail." He pulled out his wallet and counted off ten one-hundred dollar bills. "Here, this ought to take care of your deductible and any other problems that might pop up. Or not. Anyhow, have a merry Christmas."

Kay reached out and took the money, stunned that for once the hundred dollar bills in her hand belonged to her. She hadn't seen the damage to her car, but it was unlikely that it caused an issue great enough that she couldn't drive it. She looked up again and saw the man lean over and look under his truck before getting back in and hightailing it down the road in the direction he had been headed. She jumped out of her car and watched as it disappeared into the darkness of late afternoon. Even if she had thought to look sooner, she wouldn't have been able to see his license plate: it was caked over with snow. She spread the bills between her fingers, then shoved them in her coat pocket. It's just as well. At least unless he hit someone else. Nah, he didn't have booze on his breath. He was probably just distracted.

The sound of a horn blaring at her brought her back to her senses. There was a car behind hers, honking away for her to get out of the way. "Sorry," she hollered at the driver, glad that he hadn't rear ended her. She got in her car, looked both ways, then took off to her itty-bitty apartment. Safe. And not as broke as she was an hour ago.

Chapter 5

"Why, hello, Yardley," Kay said.

The cat sitting on top of the dumpster lid didn't reply but watched as Kay neared her. At the last minute, she jumped down and ran toward the snow-covered equipment-studded yard behind the shop.

"Not feeling too social today, huh, Yardley? Ah, give you a few months, and you'll be eating out of my hand," Kay said after the long gone feline.

"She's almost eating out of mine now," Jay said.

"Where'd you come from? I didn't see you when I pulled up," Kay said, trying to regain her composure after being startled.

"Well, I was born in Washington, but I just came in from the bearing store. I just needed a few things. Don't worry about losing any money on this transaction. I won't be charging the customer. These are supplies I like to have on hand in my toolbox. By the way, I know it's none of my business, but did you find a generator for Lumpy's miner buddy?"

Kay chewed back a smile. Jay didn't talk much, and now he was concerned about her personal business. "Actually, I did find a 3406B gen set. It's a 350KW, has low hours, was used as a backup unit, and only run once a month for maintenance. I got it quoted f.o.b. Anchorage dock for only $29,000. There isn't much of a warranty—only 30 days—but I figure if there's something wrong with it, it will fail pretty quick. I tried calling Lumpy this morning, but his phone went right to voice mail. Have you heard from him?"

"No, but he isn't an early riser. He doesn't live too far from here. I'll pop in and make sure nothing happened to him."

Kay tilted her head to the side, asking 'huh?'

"Lumpy had money in his pocket yesterday and the prospect of more coming his way if you found a generator for him. He may have gone on a bender. I don't think he'd fall down drunk and get hurt, but it wouldn't be a bad idea for someone—me, not you—to check on him. I'll be right back. Go on inside and get warm. I just made some coffee and there's half a box of donuts. Help yourself."

Jay jumped into his twenty-year-old white 4WD Dodge truck that now sported three different colors of mismatched hood and fenders and left the parking lot, the trail of foggy exhaust following behind him like a tail on a kite.

Kay let herself into the shop and poured herself a cup of coffee, grabbed one of the apple fritters and a paper towel, then made herself comfortable in the duct-taped office chair. She shoved aside the opened and unopened mail, parts boxes, and shop rag-wrapped oily parts, clearing a space to put her caffeine and sugar breakfast. She had been too excited to eat earlier when she had seen the email from her father's friend. 'Here's a great deal for you. Don't go too skinny on it. There's plenty of room here for you to make a good chunk of change. Have a merry Christmas, Uncle Vern.'

He wasn't her real uncle but had been looking out for her since she could remember. Actually, now that she thought about it, he was the one who started her on her way to being an entrepreneur. 'You'll never make much money working for someone else. Find out what folks want, make sure you have the sale, then get it for a good price. Mark it up a bit and make darned sure the customer is happy with the product. If something goes wrong, you gotta stand behind it, even if you lose a few bucks. Your business depends on a good reputation. People will forgive an 'Ah, shoot!' if you own up to it. Start making excuses for shoddy goods and you'll never get that customer back. And believe me, he'll tell all his friends about you, too. Now, if you do him right, he'll tell his friends about that, too. And remember, no matter what you do with your life, folks are going to see you as a woman first. Sometimes that can be to your advantage, other times, it's a liability.'

Yes, she had taken it to heart. When her job working as a parts buyer for a contracting company meant being laid off for six months out of the Alaskan year, she decided to start her own business. She had found the right niche, too. Small companies, especially those in remote areas, weren't getting the customer service they needed. A few ads placed in the right places got recurring small orders from village governments, too. They were happy to have someone who was willing to gather up goods all around Anchorage, put them into a flat rate box, and mail them to the Bush. She did learn very early to get paid before shipping, though. Taking charge cards had saved her bank account. Small local governments weren't too quick to mail out checks.

Yes, she'd only been self-employed for one year, but she wouldn't have it any other way. Plus, now she had that money from the hit and dash driver. She really couldn't call it a hit and run event since she'd been paid for the damage, but the driver did seem to be in a big hurry to leave.

Kay took another sip of coffee, then pulled out her mobile office: her smartphone. She used her laptop at home for most of her work, but she could at least keep up with emails with her phone.

After reading both of her legitimate emails, she started browsing her junk file, passing over those that didn't interest her, finally getting lost in downloading the free books of the day from several of the promotional sites she had visited months ago.

She was deep into a romantic suspense story on her Kindle app when she heard the door slam and felt the cold air hit her.

"Sorry. I didn't mean to slam the door. A gust hit it."

Jay snorted and amended his statement. "No, I really did slam it. That jerk went and got himself another DUI. That's fifteen according to the clerk downtown. Lumpy won't be going anywhere for a long time. Do you happen to have the contact information for that miner? I'd hate for you to lose the sale because he couldn't keep away from the booze."

"Um, no. Lumpy was playing it real close to the chest." She snorted in derision. "I'm sure if I had put out, he would have shared everything."

"Including herpes. He's not a clean man."

"Oh, my. Thanks for the warning, even though I didn't plan on getting close enough to catch a flea, much less an STD. Do you know if they allow visitors at the jail? Maybe I can find out something. I mean, we did have a verbal agreement to share the profits 50-50. Hopefully, he's man enough to stand on his word."

"You can try. Just remember to tell him that if you can't follow through on this sale for him, he'll get 100% of nothing. I'm sure he's never said anything around you, but he doesn't trust women."

Kay snorted. "People who don't trust aren't trustworthy. And from what little you've shared with me, it wasn't necessarily the woman's fault."

"That's neither here nor there. He tends to hang around barflies who'll do anything for a few drinks and a warm place to sleep. When he's passed out, a few of them have helped themselves to whatever they can grab, which is usually cash." Jay shook his head and changed the subject. "Go ahead and get down to the jail, but make sure you have your ID and remember to take your Leatherman out of your purse before you go in. Oh, and it wouldn't be a bad idea to have a contract ready for him to sign, giving you equal share of the profits for the generator sale."

"Got you beat on that one; I drafted a contract even before I found the generator. But thanks for the reminder about the knife. I would have forgotten that one. You've got my number, but I don't have yours."

Jay shook his head. "Don't have a cell phone, don't want one."

"Okay, then I'll call here if I need anything." Kay looked at the bulldozer at the back of the shop. "Looks like you're almost done there. I'll stop in the contractor's office and pick up the check for the parts while I'm downtown. Is there anything you need while I'm out?"

Jay paused to take in Kay's beautiful dark green eyes, her lips parted slightly in anticipation of his response. Did he need anything? Oh, to have the guts to tell her the truth! That a few minutes, hell, a few hours, of skin-on-skin time with her would be all he needed… Instead, he said, "I'm all set here. For now," and added a wink. Maybe one of these days she'd

39

see him as a man, not as a young, greasy mechanic who worked for a fast-talking drunk.

***

After signing in, showing her drivers license, and letting the desk officer know who she was visiting, Kay was finally able to relax in the waiting room. Sort of. It reeked of industrial cleansers and hopelessness, but at least she was on the outside and could leave at any time. It wasn't as if she'd be spending the holidays here, even as a visitor. Just get the contract signed, and Lumpy would be out of her life forever.

"Kay Miller?" the officer called out into the waiting room.

As so got up from the molded plastic chair, the static electricity kept her woolen scarf. "Just a minute," she said, and turned back to retrieve the last gift her grandmother had made her. "Yes, sir, officer sir, I'm Kay Miller."

"You can go in there and talk to him on the phone. The clerk said you had a paper you wanted him to sign. We have a notary here if needed. Just hand it to the her before you sit down."

Kay slipped the one-page document into the steel trough and waited while the clerk looked it over. "This is it? No power of attorney papers?"

"No, ma'am. This is strictly for a business transaction that was started…" Kay wanted to say, 'before he went out drunk driving and blew it,' but instead, cleared her throat, "That was started yesterday."

"Hmph. Most women come in here with a fistful of papers, wanting to get their man to sign over power of attorney to them so they can go and sell all his cars and property and stuff while he's in the slammer."

"Oh, no. I'm not his girlfriend or wife or anything like that. We're just business associates."

"Well," the dark-skinned matron said with a sigh of genuine relief, "That's good to hear. Lumpy spends more time in here than he does out. Watch out for him. He's slick and could talk the pelt off a grizzly bear if he wanted."

"I'll be careful. If you can witness his signature on this, though, I'd appreciate it. I don't want him coming back at me down the road, saying that I forged his name."

"That's my girl. I'll be right around. Go ahead and sit in front of him in the other room. You'll be able to see him behind the glass, but you have to use the handset for him to hear you."

Lumpy was waiting for her, all giggly and smiles like Santa was paying him a visit and had a sack full of toys.

"Hey, there, little lady. I knew you'd come see me here. I was telling all the guys in here that I had the cutest little girlfriend."

Get the paper signed first, then set him straight on relationship status. Kay took a deep breath for composure, then looked up and found her opening line. "What happened to your head. Looks like a butterfly bandage that maybe should have been stitches."

"Oh, that," he said and reached up to the gash above his eyebrow, wincing at his own gentle touch. "I wouldn't let them stitch it. They said they'd have to give me a shot to numb it first, and I won't let nobody stick a needle in me. I'm pure that way. Never a shot in my life. But anyhow, you should see the other guy!" he boasted, his chest puffed out in pride.

"Okay, as long as it doesn't get infected. Anyhow, I need to get the name and phone number of the buyer for that generator. I didn't want you to think I was going to go around you and take your sale, so I wrote up this contract. It says you'll get 50% of the profits from the sale. I just need you to put in his name and contact information, sign it, and then I can go ahead and get the ball rolling."

Lumpy took the contract from the prison clerk. "Thanks, Louella. My, my, you're looking nice today."

"Save it for someone who'll fall for your sweet talk, Lumpy. Just look over the paper, and if it satisfies you, fill in the blanks and sign it so this lady can get on her way. You only have a couple of minutes, and then we're shutting down for lunch."

"Who stepped in your grits, Louella?" he asked sarcastically, then backed down when he saw she wasn't in a joking mood. "All right, all right. Let me see."

Lumpy studied the paper, following each sentence with his index finger as he read it. "Hmm. It says you are buying the generator for $29,000 and selling it for $40,000. I think you can get at least fifty grand out of it."

"No, I can't. I want to get this over and done with. If there wasn't another gen set in the state, that'd be one thing. The Cat dealer has one for $48,000 and I know they're negotiable. Get the sale now and you can have your share in just a few days. Or whenever you get out. After all, 50% of $11,000 is better than 0% of $50,000, which is what you'd get if you got greedy."

"Ah, you're probably right. Ain't she a cute little gal, Louella?" Lumpy said, then bent to scribbling on the paper. "What is the date, anyhow?"

"November 22nd. Do you need to know the year, too, lunkhead?"

"Now, Louella, why do you talk so mean to me? Of course I know what year it is. It's just this time of year, the days go by so quickly."

Louella took the paper from him, signed her name, and stood back. "Now you got two more minutes and then this place is locking down. Say what you want and be quick about it."

The clerk looked through the security glass at Kay, rolled her eyes, then shook her head and frowned before leaving through the secured exit.

Kay smiled weakly at the silent comment about her business partner's character.

"Now that's what I want to see. I want to see you smile at me again. Go ahead, give me a great big smile. Like you'll give me when I get out of this joint. You know, they never should have arrested me. I mean, it wasn't even my car, and I'd only had a couple sips of wine with a great big dinner.

How was I to know I was going the wrong way on a one-way street when they pulled me over? The signs had snow all over them. And I couldn't let that jerk I ran into get away with calling me those names."

"I don't know anything about what happened, Lumpy. I just came in to make sure you weren't hurt, which you were, and that we got this sale going so you'd have money once you got out. Jay said you were charged with a DUI which means you'll probably need a lawyer. The profit from this may not cover all your expenses, but it's a start."

The loud obnoxious blare of the klaxon signaled that their meeting was over. "Be careful in there. I'll be in touch," Kay said, then hung up the phone and stood up.

Lumpy, evidently wanting to say more, took the phone from his ear and pointed it at her.

"Yes," she drawled into the phone.

"I love you. And I'll make this all right when I get out of here."

Suddenly, the broad body of Louella was between her and the security window. "He's getting obnoxious, isn't he?" she said. "Don't worry, he can't hear me, but be careful: he can see your face. Just wave your hand and get the heck out of here. You don't belong in a place like this, and he does."

"Thanks, Louella. You're right. I'm going right home and scrub my ears with soap and hot water. Just listening to him gives me the willies."

***

Kay bundled up with coat, scarf, and gloves before leaving the warmth of the jail into the arctic blast of yet another incoming storm. She didn't use her key to remote start her car, though, until she was standing right next to it. The Anchorage jail should be secure, but it was still in a rough neighborhood. A running car without a driver would be too much of a temptation to some, even if it was to just sit inside it and get warm.

She pulled out her notebook, scanned her to do list, and saw that the only thing left today was to get paid by the owner of the bulldozer in the shop. "Cool. Just a few blocks away."

Evidently Jay had called first, because the woman at the front desk not only knew who she was, but had the check waiting for her. "The boss said he sure appreciates the quick turnaround. We've already had a too much snow, and there's another stormfront coming in. Looks like the skiers and snowboarders are getting their prayers answered."

"And the truckers, too. There's enough snow to haul for all of them this season," Kay said. "If there's anything else you need for the yellow tractors, let me know. I don't know if the boss knows it or not, but just for the record, I don't do trucks."

The receptionist laughed. "I don't blame you. The problem with fixing trucks is that then you have to deal with the truckers. Believe me, I know enough about that. I get to give them their checks, too. You wouldn't believe the stories I hear."

"I'll take your word for it. Stay safe. Oh, and watch out for the intersections. They're especially slick."

Kay waited until she was out of sight of the contractor's office, then did a mini version of her happy dance, waving her hands in front of her chest as she neared her car. "Save the full dance until you get on solid, non-slippery ground. Next stop, the bank, then the grocery store. I'm going to load up on salad bar stuff and to heck with how much it weighs. I may even make a second container just for fruit and desserts!"

Chapter 6

The next day

"Hello, Yardley. I got you some treats. Here, I'll put them on my glove." Jay brushed off the deck of the D3 dozer with the back of his work glove, then took it off, laid it palm up, and sprinkled a few kitty snacks into it. "You don't seem too afraid of my voice. Now maybe you'll get used to my smell, too."

***

Jay walked around to the front of the shop and saw Kay's little red Sonic parked in front, the passenger side all bashed and battered.

"What happened to your ride? Take a corner a little too fast and get a bit cozy with a light pole?" he asked when he walked in and saw her waiting for him at his desk.

"Nope. Believe it or not, I was sitting at a four-way stop when some jerk came skidding through. He slammed onto his brakes, spun around a time or three, and slid into me. I was stunned, but okay. He scared the hell out of me when he came up to my side of the car. I had rolled the window down to ask if he was okay and then, bam! He wouldn't let me out. He said he couldn't take the points on his license and threw $1000 through the window to cover the damages."

"A thousand bucks won't even come close to fixing that. It might cover a partial paint job, but not replacing panels or pounding out dents and dings."

"Well, actually $500 was to cover my deductible and I think the other $500 was hush money. I can't be without the car, though. And if I file against my insurance, they're going to want to know what happened. I don't know what to say or do, so I guess I'll just drive around with my Alaska winter edition modification. I can use the money to pay down my credit cards a bit..."

Kay stopped her story when the jingle bells tied to the knob jangled, indicating that someone had come in the front door. "Hey, Jay! Got my dozer ready yet?"

Jay greeted his customer with a hearty handshake, then paused when he saw the man's face pale. He turned around to see what was causing it and saw that Kay's face was scarlet. "Do you two know each other?" he asked.

Kay snorted. "We may not know each other, but our

49

vehicles are intimately acquainted." She stood up, knuckles on her hips so she didn't strangle the man, then let loose. "You do know, don't you, that I can't report the damage to my insurance company without either a police report or getting my rates jacked up sky high."

"I'm sorry about that. I'll tell you what, you can take it down to ABC Body Repair and have them put the charges on my account."

"Yeah, right, as if they'd let someone walk in and say, 'Have so and so pay for this.' Besides, I don't have another vehicle and Alaska body shops are booked for months out at this time of year. What is your name, by the way?"

"You can call me Steve; everybody else does," he said, offering her his hand. She refused it with a snort, so he pulled it back and turned to his mechanic.

"Well, anyhow, Jay," he said, "I have some bad news for you. Lumpy's three months behind in rent and I've given him every chance I could to make it up. I even offered to let him fix that," and nodded to the tractor, "for part of it, but he refused, said he had more important, bigger money, deals in the works. Every day he says he'll get paid tomorrow, but you probably know how that goes. Anyhow, I'm evicting him. I know he's letting you stay in that little apartment around back as part of your pay, but he's supposed to be paying me for that, too. I guess that means I'm evicting you, too, buddy. I've got some guy who's wanted this place for months. He's been waiting patiently, but now he's gotta get moved in before the end of the month. And he needs the apartment, too."

"You did hear that Lumpy just got another DUI, right, Steve?" Jay asked.

"Shit! No, I didn't hear. Damn. I'm in a tight spot. I really have to get this guy moved in. Is there any way you can get his and your stuff moved out? I'm watching a place off the Seward Highway at Indian. You can use that. It ain't much, but it's dry and has a wood stove. It's up for sale, but I doubt anyone will be interested in it at this time of year. It's more of a summer site. Beautiful view of Turnagain Arm..." Steve trailed off crowing about the place he was caretaker for and asked, "So, what do you think?"

"I guess it's better than dragging everything out to the side of the road. Yeah, thanks, I'll take it. I know where that place is. By the way, your dozer will be ready to haul out tomorrow. Once it's gone, it shouldn't be too much trouble to get this place cleaned out. That is, it wouldn't be if I had a truck and trailer. Or better yet, do you still have that box truck with the lift gate?"

"Yeah, I do. You can use it. I suppose it's a good thing Lumpy's back in the slammer. If he were here, he'd be trying to talk me into another break. Not that I'd give it to him, but I'm sure you can get this place cleared out a lot quicker than he could. You're a fast mover, or so I've heard."

"Only when I want to be," Jay said, then turned to Kay and winked, "But not when it's in my best interest to be slow and thorough."

Kay blushed in response and Steve saw it. "Okay, I'm outta here," he said. "I'll send the lowboy in tomorrow. You can ride back to town with the driver and pick up the box truck."

Steve looked around and shook his head. "Sure is a lot of sh.. I mean crap in here. How he could drag this much stuff in in four months, I'll never know. Thanks for wiping his ass. Shoot, Kay, I'm sorry. Shop talk, and all."

Kay thawed at his remorse. "I'm used to it, but don't care for it, so I appreciate the apology."

"Take care. I'm sure we'll catch up again sometime. I'll make good on the repairs to your car, but you're right. Fixing it in the summer would be a better idea."

"Bye, and thanks for the loan of the box truck," Jay said as he held the door for him.

"Cool. My car may look like it went through the fluff cycle in the dryer, but Steve said he'd fix it. And he didn't ask for his money back. And even if he does want me to apply it to the repairs, at least I can play with a few extra bucks for a while."

"True. He's a good guy. He just never learned how to drive in ice and snow."

Jay plopped down in the duct-taped office chair and snagged another fritter. "Well, you really left me a big mess this time, Lumpy. Crap."

"I'll help. I mean, I'd rather not drive a truck, but get me some sturdy boxes and I'll fill them up. Oh, and have you seen that place he was talking about? You might want to make sure there's dry storage out there or there's no use in me boxing up these parts and manuals."

"There's still some daylight. Feel like a drive?" he asked.

"Sure, but I thought you had to finish the dozer."

"Like I said, I'm fast when I need to be. I got twenty hours worth of work done in about fifteen. It'll take me about twenty minutes to bolt on the guards, and then it's good to go. Your car or mine?"

"Two questions? Does yours have four-wheel drive and does your heater work?"

"Yes and yes. I'll let you help buy fuel for it, though. I haven't been paid yet and you have."

"That's the way I like it," Kay said. "Partners."

"Partners you can trust," Jay added. *And maybe bunk with.*

Chapter 7

"There she goes. There goes our Yardley," Kay said as the blob of gray bounced over the snow berms into the back yard.

He didn't want to let her know how much it meant to him to hear her refer to the feral cat as 'ours.' He'd keep quiet so he didn't scare Kay away. He didn't know much—hell, anything—about her, but a good-looking woman with a savvy business head on her shoulders and a strong sense of ethics was a rare find in a single woman. By her blushes, she was at least mildly interested in him. Like the cat, he'd get to know her bit by bit until she trusted him.

"Thanks," Kay said when he opened the truck door for her.

"Oh, wait just a minute. Let me clear out some of this garbage." Jay reached in and threw his spare hoodie and the snow broom behind the pickup seat, then gathered the assorted receipts and empty cookie bags and shoved them in the glovebox. "There, it shouldn't be too dirty. I don't think I've seen the cloth on that seat cover in months, so you're good." *Very good.*

When Jay got in the truck, Kay said, "You know, there are some women who would take exception to a man opening a car, or truck, door for them, but I appreciate it, especially in weather like this."

"Yes," Jay drawled, stretching out his reply, "And some men would be offended if a woman volunteered to help pay for fuel or dinner or whatever."

"Now, now," Kay said, pulling the scarf off her head, leaving it around her neck. "I didn't offer to buy dinner. But I will. As I said, I have a few extra bucks. When you pull in for gas, make sure it's someplace where I can get a couple of coffees or cocoas or whatever. I don't want to eat yet. Daylight hours are burning and all that jazz."

"Yes and no."

"What?"

"I'll pull in and pump while you get drinks and pre-pay, but this is a diesel. You don't want to put gas in this rig."

"You got me there. I'll be right back."

I wish I had you here. And there. And everywhere. Shoot, Jay, wake up and smell the diesel. You'd better do something or even your Carhart coveralls won't cover that boner!

"Do you have a cold," Kay asked when she got back. "You keep sniffing. And there's nothing in the air to cause hay fever."

"Nah. It's just the smell of diesel and cold air make my nose run. Nothing contagious, so don't worry."

"I'm not worried about you," she said and handed him the convenience store cappuccino.

You should be! "Thanks. Next time, I'll buy."

***

It was early enough that the traffic through town was light. The casual chit chat covered work-related subjects, like where each of them had learned their trades, but stayed away from personal subjects like exes and what the future held for them now that Lumpy was in jail.

"And here we are," Jay said as he turned off the highway on to the lightly traveled and unplowed side road. "I don't want to stop on the road, but turn around and see the view. It really is magnificent. Too bad you can't see it from the house."

"How far is it?"

"Right up there. Not even a quarter mile away from the

57

ocean."

"Are you thinking what I'm thinking, Jay?"

"Um. I doubt it. What are you thinking?"

"If there was a tsunami, we'd be wiped out."

"Nope. Definitely not what I was thinking. I have enough on my mind to worry about a once in a lifetime event."

Kay jumped out of the truck before he had a chance to open the door for her. She sloshed her way through knee-high snow to get by his side. "Now what?

"Let's go take a look around."

"Isn't it locked up?"

"Yes, it is, but Steve put Cat padlocks on everything. A good mechanic always has a Cat key on his keyring," and held up his fist-sized bundle of keys by the black-capped padlock key.

"As does a good parts lady," Kay said and jiggled her much smaller keyring at him.

She hadn't even taken two steps toward the house when he called out, "Watch your step," and grabbed her by the upper arm. "The snow's covered all sorts of stuff. Let me lead and you can walk in my footprints. Nobody's been here in a while and no telling what's under all this snow. Wait a sec. I just remembered I have a snow shovel in the back of my truck."

Kay came back and danced in place next to the pickup to stay warm while he plowed a shovel-width pathway to the house. "I got this," she said, holding up her keys, "if you want to clear a trail to that shed. That is where you're going to stash Lumpy's stuff and your toolbox, right?"

"Sure is. Go ahead inside. If you know how to start a fire, there's probably a stack of firewood inside along with a box of matches. Hopefully, there's some old newspapers, too. If not, I'll let you clean out my glovebox. Just don't burn the registration or insurance papers."

When he came in half an hour later, Kay had a fire burning and was sharpening a couple of fallen branch twigs.

"Do you have to be back to Anchorage tonight for anything special," he asked, brushing the snow off the front of his insulated coveralls.

"No, but I didn't know it was snowing. You don't think we'll get snowed in, do you?"

"I don't know, but it's coming down real heavy. I knocked most of the snow off me before I came in and I'm still covered." Jay took off his knit cap and shook it out over the sink, then laid it on the back of the wooden rocking chair next to the fire. "I know my old truck will make it, but it's getting dark fast. The roads won't be too bad for a while, but you know rush hour traffic when there's a new storm coming in. People freak out and start driving ten miles an hour."

Kay looked out the window, then over to the fire and the bag of marshmallows she had found in the cupboard. "You're not diabetic, are you?"

"What? No. Why would you ask that?"

"Because it looks like all we'll have for dinner is stale roasted marshmallows, with leftovers for breakfast. You'll have to take a raincheck on a real meal."

As long as I'm with you, sweetie. "Whatever you want to share with me will be fine." *Very fine, I'm sure.*

***

Jay looked over at the single mattress on the floor at the other side of the room. A moth-hole ridden army surplus woolen blanket and a year's worth of dust covered it. He took two broad steps across the wooden floor and yanked it off. The mattress had a fitted cotton sheet on it that looked clean and wasn't stained, and since he hadn't noticed an odor, it should be okay for the night. He stepped outside, shook the blanket out as best he could from under the eave, then came back in and tossed it to her. "I'll let you make the bed." He grabbed his hat and pulled it down over his ears. "I'll be right back," and went back into the snowstorm.

"A sleeping bag?" Kay asked when he came back in. "Did you plan this, getting stuck out here?"

"Nope," he said, ignoring her accusing glare. "I had no control over the weather. However, I always have a sleeping bag behind the seat of my truck. When I work out in the Bush, it's a necessity. There aren't any motels or bed and breakfasts in the villages. The best you can hope for is that there's an empty spot on the schoolroom floor and that their heater works. Oh, and that the wash-ateria has food. I paid six bucks for a can of chili once, and then they didn't have a microwave that worked. I didn't want to eat it cold, so I heated it on the exhaust manifold of the powerhouse generator."

"You mean the exhaust manifold of the engine for the generator."

Jay laughed and shook his head. "Yes, you're right. You know, it really is nice being around someone who can understand what I'm talking about."

"And who isn't afraid to take corrections," she said, a single nod to him.

"Or accept clarifications," Jay amended. "I knew what I meant and so did you. Now, since we're staying the night, I'm taking off my boots and getting comfortable." He unzipped his coveralls from the leg bottoms up, then stepped out of his boots. "And I'm moving this mattress closer to the fire."

Kay stood next to the kitchen sink, watching him bend over from the waist to rearrange their sleeping arrangements. Suddenly, a flush arose at the thought of them being so close together.

"Another hot flash?" he asked.

"Probably. I've only had a couple in my life, and the only decent thing about them is that they're occurring in Alaska in the wintertime. Just a minute."

Kay stepped back into her boots and stood on the narrow porch, grateful for the splattering of large cool snowflakes on her face. *You dodged another one, woman. Either that or you really are getting hot flashes. And forget about thinking that those will discourage him. He actually seems to be turned on by them.*

"Ah, instant relief," she said when she came back in.

"Ready for dinner?"

***

"I can't believe we ate the whole bag of marshmallows. You know, I think I like them better naked. I mean, better without the chocolate bar and graham crackers."

"Naked's good," Jay said softly, resisting the urge to push her hair back behind her ear.

Kay's face blazed scarlet again. "I think it's time for another hot flash break," she said and stood to leave.

Jay leaned back against the brick fireplace wall and sighed. "You know, I've noticed that the only time you have 'hot flashes' is when I've said something to embarrass you. Are you sure they aren't Jay flashes?"

"Oh, my God. Are you serious? What in the hell are those?"

"Just a phrase I just made up. I think you're leaving the room to get away from continuing an embarrassing, or otherwise sensitive, subject." He leaned forward and looked Kay in the eye. "Naked," he said and watched for her reaction.

"You did that on purpose! Of course, I'm going to blush now."

"Aha! So you admit it. Those weren't hot flashes, those were blushes. You aren't that old. At least I don't think so. Besides, age is just a number."

"That's easy for you to say. Try creeping up on forty and see how you feel. I could try lying about my age, but it wouldn't stop the years and wrinkles from accumulating."

"I'd rather have a woman of experience and kindness than one of youth and orneriness." Jay moved away from the fireplace and stood behind Kay. He put his hands on her shoulders, then lifted her hair, pausing to tuck that wayward tress of hair behind her ear. He gently pulled the scarf from around her neck and set it on the table. "This will make a nice pillow," he said, his breath soft on her ear."

I can't believe this is happening. He's so young! And so different from me. But oh how I need the stress relief! It's been too long since a man's put a hand on me that was welcomed…

"But, as I was saying, we need to get to bed. Since neither of us brought pajamas, and there wouldn't be room for both of us on that itty-bitty bed if we kept our clothes on, I think it's time to get practical."

"You mean naked," Kay said, this time welcoming the

flush.

"I'm game if you are." He pulled Kay's hoodie off over her head without resistance, then moved behind her to slip his warm hands over the front of her lacy bra, her nipples firm from both the cold and excitement. He unlatched the buckles on his coveralls and let them slip to the ground, stepping out of them, kicking them to the wall. "Making love by firelight..."

"Jay, knock it off. Just because we're going to bed naked together doesn't mean we're going to have sex."

"I know. But tell that to my little friend here."

Kay reached behind her and touched the front of his polar fleece sweatpants. "Oh, my. Geez! You win."

"What do you mean?"

"I mean, I've only been with five men in my life, and well, you win."

"Size isn't everything, darlin' Let's get started and then let me know if I win. And don't worry. I'll be gentle and slow. It may be dark out, but the night is young. We have lots of time."

"Um, I'm not a prude, but could we put your sleeping bag down on the bed first? That wool has got to be scratchy. And if we're going to be, um..."

"Naked."

"Yeah," Kay tingled at the thought, "I'd rather be on or in a sleeping bag."

"It's a good thing I'm tall and bought the extra-large size. It should fit both of us comfortably, as long as we're both snuggled close."

Jay slipped off the elastic bands that held the sleeping bag together and held it high to let it unroll.

Clunk!

"What's this?" Kay asked, holding up the large Ziploc bag with assorted sundries.

"That's my emergency kit. Go ahead and look in it. There might be something useful."

"Toothbrush, toothpaste, deodorant, Ibuprofen, Band-Aids, dental floss. Gee, it looks like the most useful items for us are the two granola bars. I guess we have breakfast covered. Too bad there isn't any coffee." Kay kept pawing through the contents. *Come on! He's a guy. There's got to be a condom.*

Jay spread the bedding out, then came and stood behind her, eager to press up against her again. He told her he'd be slow, but he didn't know it would be this difficult. She was driving him nuts without trying. "You can look through it six more times or even pour everything out on the table, but nothing else will magically appear."

"I was hoping, I mean I thought that you might have packed... I mean, if we're going to get cozy and comfortable..."

Jay leaned down and nuzzled her neck, breathing in her complex perfume of fear and anticipation. "I don't think the Trojan fairy came and put a present in there while it was in my truck. So, unless you've got some disease you want to keep me from getting, we'll be fine."

Kay pulled back. "I am not diseased! And just to be clear about things, I don't sleep around. I haven't been with a man for, for... Well, not for a long time. If I did happen to pick something up, I'm sure my gynecologist would have found it by now."

"Come here," he said and brought her close, face to face, and ran his fingers through her hair. "I'm sorry you misunderstood me. I would never take you for a woman of loose morals. And just for the record, my ex-wife and two girlfriends had a bet. They all went off the pill and wanted to see which one of them I'd get pregnant first. Of course, I didn't find out about it until a year later. Oh, and by the way, I'm the one who won. None of them got pregnant. It wasn't until two years later that they all started having babies, and by then I was long gone, all the way up here to Alaska. So, even if your hot flashes aren't the real deal, we'll be fine."

"Oh, okay. I guess. No, wait! You were sleeping with three women at the same time?"

"Not at the same time as in we were all in the same room. I was estranged from my wife, but she came by to, ahem, get a little every once in a while. I was dating two of the other women who worked at the bar with her, too. It was casual and usually involved a bit too much Yukon Jack, but no one was hurt. I was just a kid. They wanted me for my body and the little trinkets I'd sometimes buy them. Of course, whenever I did get gifts, I had to make sure to get three and all of them the same."

"You don't have any girlfriends or wives waiting somewhere for you now, do you?"

"Nope. It's just me. Looks like I'll only have to buy one present at a time now."

Kay sighed, put her hands around his neck and whispered, "You talk too much for a quiet guy," and kissed him thoroughly.

Chapter 8

"Hey, sleepyhead. Ready to head into town?"

Kay started to sit up, then remembered where she was and what she had been doing the night before—and with whom—then lay back on the pillow made of her wadded-up scarf. "Do we have to go so early? It's not even light yet."

"Ha ha," Jay said dryly. "I'd rather spend all day in bed with you, but I told Steve I'd have his dozer ready to load onto the Lowboy by daylight. If we leave now, and the traffic isn't horrendous, I'll have an hour to put it all back together."

"Can you call him and tell him it'll be a bit longer? That you ran into a…a… snowstorm?"

"I could if a phone would work out here. We're in a dead zone and cell phones won't work. Besides, he knows where I am and probably guessed we were coming out together. I wouldn't want to impugn your integrity."

"Say what?"

"Cell phones don't work out here."

"No, I mean about my integrity?"

"I mean, I wouldn't want to tarnish your reputation. Make

you look like a wanton woman, whatever. Shoot. Never mind. But we have to get out now. Who knows what the traffic will be like, plus there's bound to be snow plows on the road, too."

"I know what impugn means, and it's very gallant of you to be looking out for me, but I'm a grown woman and I can do what I want, with whomever I want…as long as we're not married. I mean, to someone other than each other. I mean… Shoot! I shouldn't try to speak so early in the morning. The words don't fit together right, dang it!"

"Do whatever it is you need to do in the bathroom then lock the door behind you. I'm going to warm up the truck and knock the snow off. Don't worry, though. We'll have enough time to swing by and get a couple of coffees. And maybe some fresh donuts. Those granola bars are about two years old."

***

"It's a good thing we left when we did and that all the roads to the shop are on the main drags. Shoot, we made better time than if it was summer."

Kay took another sip of her now cold coffee and nodded her head in agreement. They probably would have had time for a quickie. *Don't worry about it, woman. He doesn't seem to care for quickies and as it is now, you can barely keep your legs together. Start packing while he's working to keep your mind off him and what went on last night. And could happen again tonight. Damn! Don't obsess about a man. It was just sex. Great sex, but still just sex.*

"Here," Jay handed her the taper and pointed to the stack of flattened boxes. "I'm pretty sure you know how to use a tape gun. Go ahead and start boxing the service manuals and parts books first, then the smaller boxes of parts and filters; stuff we don't want to get wet on the ride over in the pickup. It won't take long to get this buttoned-up, and then I can dig out those wire baskets and start tossing the hard parts into them."

An hour later, the bells on the door jingled and Steve walked in, carrying two large coffees. "I figured you'd still be here, helping Jay get things sorted for Lumpy. I can't tell you how much I appreciate it, but thought I'd start with a couple of hot coffees, or rather mochas." He handed one to Kay. "If you don't have a sweet tooth now, Kay, you're sure to get one soon if you hang around this guy too much longer."

Jay walked up to him and accepted his drink. "All done.

Do you want a handwritten bill for this? It was only two grand for my part."

"Ach. Go ahead and scribble out a bill, but make it for $2200." He started counting out hundred-dollar bills. "Consider it a bonus for getting it done so fast, plus suggesting I get parts from Kay. She really does know her stuff. I'd pay a lot more from Cat for those parts, plus she got them to you mighty fast. Here," he said and peeled off two more bills from his roll, "you get a tip, too."

"You really don't have to," Kay said, but Steve stopped her with a head shake.

"I'd rather spend my bucks with you two. You really ought to get a business going together."

"Yeah," Jay said as he looked up from his notepad. "I was thinking that, too. We'll see. I don't necessarily need a shop since I'm comfortable doing Bush work, and having someone to source the parts and maybe, in the future, do my billing, makes the idea mighty appealing." He tore the sheet of paper from the tablet, "Here you go. Maybe next time it will be a printed copy, one your secretary can read."

"Kay, since this bad boy here refuses to get a cell phone, would you give me your number? Oh, and by the way, Jay, you can stay out there at Indian for as long as you want. It's been on the market for over a year now, and as long as you don't trash the place—and I know you won't—it's free for you. And to anyone else you care to have share that small little cabin with," he added with a wink at Kay.

Were they that transparent! Pull yourself together, girl!

"Speaking of numbers," Kay said and handed him her desktop-published business card, "Can I get yours? I'm sure Jay has it, but he won't always be around." *Liar, liar! At least, you hope he'll be!*

Steve handed her his business card. "I've got a lot of equipment, but not all of its Cat. Can you source other vendors?"

"Yes, I can. If I can't, I'm not afraid to say so. But I do love a challenge."

"Well, you'll have one soon, I'm sure. Good luck out there at Indian, you two. There's no electricity, but there is an old diesel generator if Jay can get it going."

Jay held up a can of starting fluid. "If I can't, I'll see if I can do a little resuscitating, me and my little friend here."

"Shoot!" Kay said. "Excuse me, guys, but I have to get back with that gold miner." She looked at her watch. "He told me to call at ten, and it's five after."

"Brock's cool, so don't worry about him. Oh, and you don't have to worry about him getting all feely-grabby with you, either. He's a happily married man. Tell him I said hi," Steve said. "And I'll just show myself to the door. My driver will be here in about ten minutes, so bundle up, Kay. It takes a while to get the dozer out the door."

As soon as he was gone, Kay was on the phone. She was doing her best to pay attention, but Jay was bent over just a few feet away, pouring out cat food into an automatic feeder. *Such a cute bottom, and it was all mine last night!*

"Oh, yes. Thank you, Brock. I'll get an invoice ready for you and put my wire transfer routing information on it. Or you can deposit it into my checking account if you have a branch up there. Oh? You're in Fairbanks today? Cool, I'll just put my bank account number on the invoice. Just put it in the checking account. That'll save some time. The generator is in the Midwest, but as soon as I get your funds and transfer them to my source back there, they'll get the generator on the road to Seattle. Depending on which sailing it makes, I expect it to be here in ten days or less. I've got your number, so I'll keep you updated. Oh, and I'll just take a picture of the invoice if it's easier for you since you're on the road. Yes, you're right. How'd we ever do business before smartphones and the internet."

When Jay came back in from feeding the cat, Kay was finished with her call and busy creating an invoice. "I'm glad I left my laptop here yesterday. So, how's Yardley?"

"She saw me and came running out from under that orange connex. She still won't get too close, but she knew I had food. I put the dish out under the eave out back. I'll tell Steve about her and leave some food, and hope he remembers to feed her. Even if he doesn't, she's been living the feral life for a while and didn't need me before. She's tough and can do fine without me."

I did fine without you, too, and now all the sudden, I'm wanting you to take care of me. "Well, sometimes a female *can* take care of herself, but *wants* a male around. At least, you. I mean… Steve may be able to put out food, but you'll always be special to her."

Jay pulled her close, kissed the top of Kay's head, and said, "You're special to me, too."

***

"I can't believe we got that much done in two days," Kay

said, kicking back in one of the few items that remained in the shop, the duct-taped chair. "Generator sale completed, money in the bank, your stuff, the whole shop, and Lumpy's messes all boxed up and taken out to the new shop…"

"Two days and two nights," Jay amended. "I really didn't plan on 18-hour days with this. I'd rather spend my evenings, nights, hell, early mornings, noons, and afternoons with you, getting to know you better," he smiled and nearly blushed at the thought of all the ways he wanted to get to know her, "but the sooner we're out of here, the better."

"So, you think I should go ahead and give notice on my apartment? I talked to the landlord about it and he said he'd be fine if I wanted to leave at the end of the month. He wouldn't dun me as long as the place was clean enough for the next tenant."

"It's up to you, but I don't see a problem with us living together. I mean, yes, we do fine working together, and we'd be in each other's face—and hopefully many other places—all day and night. I'm *up* for it if you are."

"There you go again, trying to make me blush…or making me blush. So, other than this chair and that box of Lumpy's office crap, we're all packed, right?"

"All swept out and ready to go."

"All right. Go ahead and drive out to Indian and I'll meet you out there. I'll stop by and pick up something for dinner, too."

***

"Ah, it's so nice to have a fire blazing when I come home, I mean…"

"It's okay to call it home," Jay said, as he came over to take the plastic tote from her.'

"Well, I guess it's both home and office. I guess it could be used as a shop, too, if you decide to tear down and rebuild a carburetor or turbo on the kitchen table." Kay took the bag of tacos and burritos off the top of the tote. "But for right now, this is a dinner table. I've never cooked on an open fire before, but I'm already getting tired of fast food. At least we don't have to worry about having a refrigerator or freezer. I'm sure that once you get the shop set up, you'll have time to mess with that old generator."

"Here, have a seat," Jay said and pulled out the kitchen chair. "Now close your eyes. I have a surprise."

Kay sat down and covered her eyes. "It isn't going to bite me or anything, is it?"

"Nope. Just keep your eyes closed."

"Hey! I hear music. Did you get batteries for that old shop radio?"

"Nope. Now open them."

"Whoa! Light!" Kay stood up and looked around her. "Actual honest-to-goodness, not a candle or Coleman lantern, light. And is that a humming from the shop I hear?"

"Yup. It didn't take more than a whiff of starting fluid to get that old generator fired up. And the day tank was full, too. I'd say it'll last a week if we only run it at night. For an hour or two. I was kinda getting used to eating and snuggling by candlelight," Jay said, then gathered her close. He kissed her gently, then pulled back. "And I don't think we need any heat other than the fireplace and what our bodies will make with a bit of friction and shared body warmth. Now, as much as I'd like to start with making heat with you, I'm famished. Let's eat before it gets colder."

"I'm with you on that," she said, then divvied up the dinner.

"So," Jay said as he reached for a third taco, "When do I need to get back to town to pick up your furniture?"

Kay laughed, then wiped the burrito juice from the side

of her mouth. "You see that tote? That and the suitcase of clothes still in the car are all I have. My apartment came furnished. All I had for personal kitchenware was an electric skillet, a couple of plates, bowls, and cups, and a saucepan. The landlord looked the place over, saw it was ready for the next guy, and gave me my deposit back. I guess there's a big to do going on up at Alyeska in December, and he's wanting to do a little price scalping. I really don't care. I have a few more bucks in the bank account. If my windfalls keep up, I may be out of debt in five years, not twenty."

Thump! Thump! Thump!

"Who could that be?" Jay said, and jumped up to answer the door.

"What are you doing, hanging out at my place?" Lumpy asked with a big 'I got you now' grin on his. "Oh, I see you have a nice fire going. And dinner? No, thanks. I already ate. Besides, Mexican food gives me gas."

"How? What, what are you doing out of jail? The bail was so high, I thought you'd never get out," Jay said, moving to stand in front of Kay, his arms behind him to keep her safe, just in case.

"Jerry put up the bail and said he'd stand for me as a

third-party."

Kay looked around Jay. "What's a third party?"

Jay answered, "It means you have someone with a good reputation who'll keep you next to him, or at least within earshot, for twenty-four hours a day to make sure you don't screw up again. So, where is Jerry? And how'd you get out here?"

"Oh, I got some wheels. And Jerry said he had to get some business taken care of in Whitehorse, but he'd be back in a few days." Lumpy turned to face Kay. "Oh, and by the way, Whitehorse is in Canada. How's it been going for you, little lady? This guy with the teensy feet been trying to keep you warm at night?"

Lumpy's snide light-hearted banter turned cold and viscous. "So, where's my money? You didn't spend it all on pretties for yourself and *him*, did you?" Thumbing towards Jay.

Jay pushed Kay back behind him and stood inches from Lumpy's face. "What in the hell are you doing here? Steve gave us permission to stay here until this place was sold. You're trespassing."

Lumpy pulled a piece of paper out of his pocket. "No,

you're the ones who are trespassing. I bought this place a few hours ago. See, all signed, nice and pretty. It just has to be recorded, and that will take a few days. So, I'm giving *you*," he stabbed Jay in the middle of the chest with his index finger twice, "an eviction notice. She can stay for as long as she wants. You do want to stay here, don't you, little lady? I mean, we have so much potential, you and me. I'll find the buyers and you can help find the goods, take care of the paperwork, take care of me…and my big feet." Lumpy lifted his oversized snow boot, displaying it as if it was covered in gold.

"I don't think so. I've made other business arrangements. Jay, would you help me gather my stuff and escort me to my car?"

Jay backed away from Lumpy and said, "If you ever touch me again, it'll be the last thing you do, at least with all your appendages. I'm not afraid to go back to jail, but when and if I do, it'll be for a good reason, not because I succumbed to the call of a bottle of vodka."

"Eww, eww," Lumpy said, his hands in the air in mock surrender.

Kay gathered the few clothes she had left in the house

and threw them in a shopping bag. "Come on, let's go. I'm ready."

Jay handed her her coat, put on his, and picked up the blue plastic tote that held nearly all of Kay's worldly possessions. *How could he have let her down so quickly? Now what?*

The two proceeded to her car in silence. "At least it isn't snowing," she said as she hit the remote start and opened the back door for Jay.

He shook his head and smiled at her. "You know, that's one of the things I like most about you. You always find a bright side to everything. Where are you going?"

"Shit. I don't know. And what do you mean 'you going?' Aren't you coming, too?"

"Not until I have all my stuff out of that lean to. He'd have my tools sold in a heartbeat if I wasn't around. I'll go in and gather my sleeping bag and what not, and sleep in the truck. Don't worry. He won't hit me."

Kay started giggling. "You were right. You never know when you're going to need that sleeping bag and toiletries."

"What bothers me most is why Steve never told us what was going on. He could have at least given us a heads up,"

Jay said.

Kay sat in the driver's seat, took out her cell phone, and looked at the second screen. "Shit. There's a voice mail. I don't know if I can retrieve it or not, but," she scrolled through the call list. "Yup. I missed a call from Steve and he left a voice mail. I guess I should have pulled over to listen to it. He must have called when I was doing the final walk through and getting paid by the landlord. Shit!"

"Now, that's three times I've heard you cuss since I've known you and all in the last minute. Don't let this get to you. I'm not sure what's going to happen, but missing that phone call just let us have an extra hour or two together."

"I just wished we hadn't wasted it on Taco Bell," Kay said, then started laughing and crying at the same time. "I gotta go. Don't let him get to you. He seems bent on pushing your buttons, and no matter what you say, I don't want you going to jail. Again."

"You're not getting out of here that quick. Come here." He reached in and helped her out of the car, then bent to kiss her.

"Wait, whoa. Won't Lumpy see us?"

"Lord, I hope so. Maybe then he'll stop hitting on you."

He kissed her deeply, grinding his loins up against hers, letting her know that he wanted more than his tongue inside her. "Us getting kicked out of our home, even if we were essentially squatting, is just a temporary setback. Drive carefully."

"Okay," she said meekly.

Life had felt so right for her the past couple days. She'd never let a man dominate her, but she'd let Jay be in charge any day. She felt safe with him.

Chapter 9

December 23

How could she have been so naïve. It had been six weeks and not a word from him. It was time to bite the bullet and call Steve and see if he knew where Jay was.

"Good afternoon. Is Steve in today?"

"No, he's not. He's on vacation. May I help you or take a message?" the receptionist asked.

"Just tell him Kay called in to see if he needed anything."

"Kay? Kay the parts lady?"

"Um. Yes."

"Oh, great. He was hoping you'd call. He lost your phone number and has some projects he wanted to get started on after the first of the year. Let me get your number and I'll give it to him when he checks in."

"Cool. Thanks." Kay gave her the number, then hung up and did the happy dance. "Money, money, money!" she sang. "Finally!"

Kay stopped dancing when the phone rang. "This is

Kay."

"Oh, my God, Kay. You are the hardest person in the world to get in touch with. Of course, for some stupid reason my receptionist thought your name was Karen and she kept looking all over the internet for Parts by Karen, or some such nonsense. Actually, I'm not sure how she was looking it up, but she recognized your voice when you called. Hey, are you still in the parts business?"

"Yes, I am. Can I help you with something?"

"Just give me your email and I'll send you the scanned parts lists. Go ahead and get everything coming. I won't need it until after New Years, so bring it in accordingly. And if you need money up front, just put together a pro forma invoice and get it to Alice, the receptionist. I think she has a little crush on you, by the way. I didn't want to break her heart and tell her you didn't play for her team, so be nice to her, but don't lead her on."

"Oh, okay. Thanks. And have a merry Christmas, wherever you are."

"We're in Hawaii and believe it or not, I'm missing the snow. My wife isn't and all she has to do to distract me is to put on that itsy-bitsy bikini of hers and I'm all for warm

Christmases. I'll see you in a week or two! Aloha!"

Kay hung up the phone, opened her laptop, and started looking for the email. Refresh. Nope. Not yet. "Give it a minute, woman." Refresh. "Ah, there you are. Cool. One, two, four parts lists! Money, money, money!" she sang again.

It wasn't until she had finished her last spreadsheet of part numbers, suppliers, and costs that she realized she hadn't remembered to ask Steve if he'd heard from Jay.

Why are you even thinking about him? True, the physical part of the relationship was off the charts fantastic, and he was a considerate and respectable man, and those bulky clothes hid that 'so much better than the statue of David' body, but you weren't in love with him. "Yeah, but I sure had a serious case of being in like with him," she said aloud as she shut the laptop.

"Dang dark winters," she said when she looked out the south-facing window of her puny rent-by-the-week hotel window. "And it's only four o'clock. I don't care. I'm tired and going to bed. I'll call Mom tomorrow and wish her a merry Christmas.

***

January 2

"Wow. I didn't know these would take up so much room. Let's see. If I combine all these parts into this box, and make two trips to Steve's, I should be able to make room for the rest of the parts that are coming in this afternoon."

Kay got out her box knife and opened, checked off, and rearranged the contents of the twelve boxes Fed Ex had brought to her down to three boxes. "Cool. I only need to make one trip. Good grief, how pathetic is this. The highlight of my day is sorting tractor parts." She chuckled out loud. "No, all these parts mean money coming in. Money, money, money!" she sang again, and finished taping the boxes.

***

Kay pulled up in front of the construction company and headed in with just the invoices. "Hi, there, Alice. I have some of the parts Steve ordered and an invoice. Where can I take them?"

"We can put them in the back room for now. When the guys come in tomorrow, I'll have them take them out to the shop. Here, let me give you a hand. You look a little beat. I mean, you look great, but are you feeling okay? You need to start taking some vitamins or something. You're getting dark circles under your eyes and you're too young for those. Oops. Sorry if I'm being too familiar."

"No, no. You're fine, but I will take a hand. I may have made one of these too heavy."

"Which is the heavy one?" Alice asked. I'm a body builder and love a challenge."

"Am I in time to help?" Steve asked as he came out the front door. "Sorry, I should have come out earlier, but was on a phone call." He looked at Kay and smiled, then frowned. "Come inside and I'll help Alice with the rest of these. You don't look too good."

Kay grimaced but didn't say a word. Did she really look that bad? She hadn't felt like eating lately, but hadn't been sick, just tired. Maybe Alice was right and she should start taking vitamins.

Alice walked in with the one heavy box and Steve carried the other two. "Alice, get a check ready and I'll sign it. Not that I'm trying to kick you out the door or anything, Kay." He came over and sat in the chair next to her. "What's wrong?"

"Why do people keep saying I look sick or puny or whatever? Maybe I'm just showing my age," Kay said, hoping the irritation she was feeling didn't come through her voice.

"Let me look at your eyes," Steve said, and held her hand at the same time. "Hmm. I've seen this before. You got me those parts for the dozer before Thanksgiving, right?"

"Yeah. What does that have to do with anything?"

Steve whispered in her ear. "I think you're pregnant."

"What?" Kay screeched and pulled back.

"Babies. They happen to the best of us. I just found out I'm going to be a father again while we were in Hawaii. You have that same look. If you were my wife or daughter, I'd tell you to first, get to the store and buy some pre-natal vitamins, then call and make an appointment with an obstetrician." Steve saw the shocked, then sad look on her face. "Don't tell me. You don't have insurance and you haven't heard from Jay since Lumpy got out of jail."

"Okay. I won't tell you. You seem to know everything already, anyhow."

"Damn! I wish I knew where that kid was. He's a good man, don't get me wrong, but after Lumpy went after him with the shotgun, he fell off the radar. But you're a tough one. You'll make it. And I'll throw all the business I can your way. And I'll spread the word, but only to folks I know who'll pay you. I'm pretty sure you'll qualify for Medicaid, so get working on that right away."

Steve looked back and saw that Alice was waiting for him to sign the check. "Here," he said and scrawled his signature, "and this is my private cell number. I noticed you had a receipt from a hotel in the front seat of your car. Go find a decent apartment or duplex and I'll help you get in to it. You know, do any heavy lifting, first and last month's rent and security deposits, that sort of thing."

Kay bowed her head, ashamed of the tears that were welling up. "Hey," Steve said. "I may be finally getting that daughter I always wanted. If I wasn't around to help her when she needed it, I'd hope that someone like me would be there to get her out of a bind."

"Thanks, I appreciate it." She wiped her nose with the back of her coat sleeve. "All right. First to the store for vitamins and a pregnancy test, then I'll let you know about the housing. I'm still not sure that I haven't had a period because I'm starting menopause."

"Pfft! You're too young and um, I mean…" Steve was embarrassed and just waved the rest of the comment away. "Let me know when you find that apartment. I want to check it out and make sure it's in a safe neighborhood."

Kay waved the check he had given her in the air, "Until then, I'll do my best to pay my own way," then walked out of the building, headed to the bank and pharmacy.

As she pulled away, Alice walked out to stand next to Steve. "So, you didn't tell her that Jay was working for you out on Shemya?"

"No, and don't you tell her, either. If he were closer, I'd kick his ass. Her pregnancy is between the two of them."

"No," Alice said. "It's between you and Kay. I don't think Jay knows about it." Steve glared at her. "But don't worry, I won't tell him. But I think someone should."

Chapter 10

Early June

"I don't believe you, and what are you doing, calling me?"

"Now, Jay, you and I got along just great before Kay came into the picture. I got some big jobs lined up here in Anchorage. Why don't you come on back and help me get some of these old engines put back together? Kay has herself another man now, anyway. You should see her, all swelly-belly, hanging on to that big dude. I think he's a doctor or something."

"You're a liar, Lumpy. If words are coming out of your mouth, they're lies."

"Hey, if you don't believe me, just call around to some of your old vendors. She's still working. I guess that husband of hers wants her to quit, him being a doctor and all, but you know her. Little Miss Independence wants to work and earn her own way."

Lumpy was grinning from ear to ear. He may have

missed his former mechanic with that old shotgun, and those lazy good-for-nothings that he hired to rearrange the features on Jay's face wound up in the ER after he fought back and stopped them with his snow shovel, but getting back at him with lies and making him hate Kay was even better. He knew he didn't have a chance to get into Kay's pants, but now Jay wouldn't get back into them, either.

***

"I need to order an o ring kit, some bearing mount, and has that parts gal Kay come in lately?"

Jay slapped his forehead, realizing how lame he sounded. Couldn't he have worked it into the conversation with any finesse at all?

"What size range on the o rings, and yeah, Kay was in here yesterday. She looks like she's going to pop any day, but says she has another month to go."

Click!

"Hello? Hello? What in the heck was that about? Geez."

***

"Steve, Jay just called in," Alice said as she stuck her head into his office.

"Good. I've been wanting to talk to him. He's the hardest

person to get in touch with. If he didn't always get back to me via fax, I'd can his ass," Steve said. "Come on in. What'd he say?"

"Well, he sounded out of sorts, like he was in a bind or something. Kinda crazy, if you know what I mean. He wasn't making any sense. He said he hated to do it to you, but he had to quit. I asked if he wanted to talk to you about it; that you'd find a way to make things work out, but he said no and hung up."

"He didn't leave a number, did he?"

"No, sir. And the caller ID said private. I don't even know if he was calling from the job site. You don't think he got in trouble, do you?"

"No more than he's already in. And of course, he'd have to do it in the middle of summer when every mechanic worth even half his wages is working somewhere else. Let me make a few phone calls and see if I can get a replacement. And call that job foreman and see if you can find out what in the hell is going on!"

***

"No, sir. I was in the field office when he came in from out at the crusher to make a phone call. Right after that, he came in and told me he had to quit, sorry for the inconvenience, then scribbled his hours on an old envelope and said to direct deposit his pay like we have been." The job foreman pulled the phone from his ear. "You don't need to yell. I may be all the way out here in the Aleutians, but the land lines here work just fine. No, I didn't ask who he called or what went on. I didn't get a chance. He split so fast, he forgot his heavy coat. But not that damn cat. He did take her.

"Anyhow, I went back and hit redial on the phone he'd used. It was the bearing house. When I asked if Jay had just called an order in, they said the only call they had in the last hour was some crackpot looking for o ring kits who'd hung up. Sorry, Steve, but I don't think he's coming back. Hey, does that mean you'll hire my nephew?"

"Can he lift eighty pounds and does he know the difference between AC and DC?"

"Yes, sir. And what he doesn't know, I'll show him. Still, it would be nice to have Jay back. I was sorta getting used to that mangy gray cat of his, too. She was the best mouser around. Shoot, she'd even take on rats as big as she was!"

***

You imbecile. Now what are you going to do? Take an

assumed name? Crap. Who are you hiding from and why? So, she broke your heart. It's your own damned fault for not calling her. How was she supposed to feel? It's not as if she was just a weekend fling, or an old girlfriend you popped in on when you got the hornies. You and Kay had a future planned. Maybe not in detail, but nothing could stop you two from creating a great business. She was someone you could trust. And now she went and married some doctor and is going to have his kid. To quote Kay, 'Shit!'

***

"Steve, do you think your wife would let you take me to the hospital? I know she's only been home a couple weeks, but I think it's time."

"Really, Kay? I mean, of course she will. She and the baby are fine. Oh, and thanks for that cute little kuspuk you made for Lily. Who would have thought to make a snuggle blanket like that? Keeps her bare little head warm when nursing. Oh, sorry. I'll be right over. You do have your bag ready, right?"

"Ooh. Ouch. Yeah, robe and slippers. I'm set. The sooner you get here, the better, but don't run any red lights."

***

"Hey, weren't you in her just last week with another pregnant woman?" the lady at admitting asked Steve.

"It was two weeks ago, but yes, I was. That lady was my wife. This is my, my friend," he said with a flush.

"He's one of my customers and the father couldn't be here, so he's stepping in," Kay said and handed her the pre-registration papers.

The wrinkled crone behind the desk snorted in derision, and shuffled the papers to delay the sign in process. *Another whore and her john.*

Kay saw the sneer and realized what she thought she had meant. "He's not that kind of customer! And you shouldn't be so quick to judge. Now, can you speed it up and get me up to labor and delivery before I make a mess in this wheelchair." Kay bent forward and started deep breathing. "Crap!" she said when her contraction was over.

"You'd better do as she says. This is her first child, but her pains are coming every couple of minutes. I should know. Like I said, I just went through this. And even if she was a woman of the streets, that baby needs to come into this world with dignity, not derision. Now, snap to it, granny. Your bosses take customer complaints seriously, especially from contractors who are building the new wing."

"All this seems in order. Go right through the doors. You know the way."

"And she didn't even say she was sorry," Steve grumbled as he speed-walked to the nurses station. "They're two minutes apart, so just point out which room and I'll get her in there."

"Mr. Stephanovich? Weren't you here just last week?" the nurse said, taking over pushing the wheelchair.

"Yes, but that was my wife. This is someone who is very close to both myself and my wife, so I'd appreciate it if you let me hang around. You know I've been through the birthing classes and shit!"

Steve recognized the grimace on Kay's face and grabbed the first thing he could find to contain the puke: the plastic-wrapped bed pan. He ripped it open and held it under her chin, supporting her back with his other hand. "It's okay. Let it out…"

When Kay was finished, she wiped her mouth with a wad of tissues. "Not exactly for the right end, but waste from one end or the other, captured and not running down the front of me…"

Kay's jaws clenched, and she leaned forward as another contraction hit.

"Breathe, honey. In slowly, out slowly. That's my girl. Nurse," Steve squinted to see the name tag, "Donna, I may not have your experience, but I'd say she's ready. I'm going to leave the room so you can check her."

He turned to Kay. "I'll be just outside the door. Holler if you need me, or need anything, or well, I'll be right here."

Tears started flowing at his words. "I'm glad someone is here. I never thought I'd have a child, and even if that miracle happened, I didn't want to be raising her alone."

"You won't be alone. My wife and I may not be blood, but we're family, just the same. And your little one will have a cousin waiting for her when she does show. Now, lie back and do what the nurse tells you."

The nurse had been busy while Steve gave his pep talk, taking blood pressure, temperature, and wrapping the fetal monitor belt around her. "Okay, you got a contraction coming. I'm going to check your dilation."

"Yeow!" Kay huffed and puffed and blew and almost cussed, but knew that breaking the breathing regimen would make the pains worse. Or so Mrs. Steve had told her.

"Hold tight and don't go anywhere," the nurse said with a smile. "Mr. Stephanovich, you can come in now. You were right. It won't be long. I'm paging her doctor now."

"Ow! Son of a bitchin' whore mongorin'…" Kay held her breath, but her mind went on and on with a string of swear words directed at the pain.

"Go ahead and cuss some more if you want," Steve said, holding her hand. "But stop holding your breath. Those deep breaths are pumping oxygen right to the baby, so stop holding *her* breath."

Kay panted quickly, then took a deep breath. "Why does it have to hurt so much?" she asked, tears streaming down her face.

Steve looked down at his hand, red from when she had squeezed it during the last contraction. "It doesn't hurt *that* much…"

Kay let go of his hand and flipped him off, then started panting with another contraction.

When it was over, Steve stood up, "I'll be right back," then rushed to the nurses station. "Someone with some skills better come in here quick or I'm going to have to catch this baby."

Three nurses leapt up while the fourth remained on the phone. "I'm trying to find the doctor now. She's supposed to be in the hospital, but no one knows where."

Steve nearly ran into the red-haired woman when he turned into Kay's room. "Who are you?" he asked the lady dressed in culottes and a tank top.

"I'm her doctor. Grab me one of those gowns, would you, and I'll scrub up."

Steve pulled the gown from the cabinet and put it over his arm and went back to hold Kay's hand through another contraction. "He doesn't know what he's missing," he said. "I promise you, she's going to be beautiful. Thank you for letting me be here with you."

Kay huffed and puffed again, then leaned forward. 'Bed pan,' she whispered hoarsely.

Steve stood up to grab the correct container as the doctor grabbed the gown from his arm.

"You're okay. Barfing's good. It just means it's time. How's it looking there, Doc?"

While Kay had been puking, the doctor had gloved up and was performing her examination. "She's ready. Are you the father? You sure look familiar."

"No, I'm a close friend. The father couldn't be here. Do you have enough light?"

"I got this," the nurse who had just come in the room said. "Would you move over to the other side, please? Kay, I've set up this mirror. Can you see her head yet?"

"Oh, my God! Is that her? Oh, crap! Again..." and she started panting.

"Work you magic, Doc. I got this end," Steve said as he wiped Kay's brow with a damp washcloth. "Just another minute..."

The nurse looked up and noticed the beginning of a swoon. "Hey, Mr. 'I'm not the dad but just a friend,' you need to breathe, too."

Steve took a deep breath and looked down at Kay. "Don't take this wrong, but God, you're beautiful."

"All new mothers are," the doctor said. "Here she is," and held her up for a quick look. "The cord was wrapped around her neck, but she's find. Let us wipe her down and do a couple of checks, and then she's all yours."

"All mine?" Kay gazed at the white vernix-covered baby and started sobbing. "She sure is. And you're right, Steve. She's beautiful."

Chapter 11

Steve had fessed up the day after the baby was born. "I knew where he was up until about a month ago. He went to work for me out in Shemya. I made sure your phone number was pasted all over the office for when he needed to order parts. Or just talk to you. If I brought your name up in the course of business, like 'Make sure you get these parts from Kay,' he'd get all flustered and leave for some reason or another. When he did have a parts order, he made sure someone typed up the list before sending it to you. 'I got lousy handwriting,' he'd say. I know now that he knew you'd recognize his writing."

Kay shrugged at the admission, then went back to stroking her baby's sparse hair.

"He made me promise not to tell *anyone* he was working for me. He did have a valid reason, though. There was an assault on him before I gave him the job out of town. Word on the street was there was a contract out on him."

"What?" Kay said a little too loudly, startling the baby. "There, there, darling. I'm sorry. I just heard something that upset me. We'll be fine." She turned her attention back to Steve and lowered her voice, "Now what were you saying?"

"Me and my big mouth. But I guess it's moot now. He's gone so far off the radar, he might as well be working in another solar system."

"Or out in the Bush for cash," Kay said. "I hear a lot of guys do that to keep from paying child support."

"Kay, did you ever tell him you were pregnant?"

"You know I didn't. I haven't talked to him since the day we parted company at Indian, when Lumpy came back and kicked him out, telling him I could stay, pretty much on the condition that I'd put out." She got up and put the baby in her bassinet. "Now, did *you* tell him I was pregnant? I mean, you pretty much knew about it before I did."

"No, I figured that was your business. I had no idea he'd stay incommunicado for so long. Actually, I thought he might have been calling you in the evenings, but just didn't want anyone to know about it."

"Okay, I believe you, but do me a favor. If you see or hear of him, would you let him know I really, really need to talk to him."

"Yes, ma'am. You have my word. And if he tries to

weasel out of it, I have a taser and I'm not afraid to use. I'll zap him and drag him to you if I have to."

Kay giggled. "Thanks. I needed that. Now, if you don't mind, I'm going to take a nap. Or even if you do mind. Having a baby sure takes a lot out of you. I'm still exhausted."

"Before I go, if you're not going anywhere today or tomorrow, can I borrow your car?"

"Yeah. Sure. I don't need anything at the store. I'm set. All I want to do is sleep, maybe eat one of those big man-sized TV dinners and have an apple for dessert and take care of this baby."

"Well, I'm glad you let me forward your calls to my office for this week, at least. And remember to drink lots of milk."

"I know, I know. I have to drink milk to make milk. Or something like that. Good night, or good afternoon, or whatever time it is. See you in two days."

***

Knock, knock. "Are you awake?" Steve called softly.

"Yeah, come on in. We're just watching a movie." Kay sniffed the air. "Ooh, what did you bring me. I know it's something to eat. Fried chicken?"

"Nope. Roasted chicken. It's better for you. But I did

splurge and picked up some twice-baked potatoes and a dish of custard for dessert. And a big container of carrot and raisin salad. Oh, and a loaf of fresh-baked multigrain bread. Except for the custard, you should have lots of leftovers, plenty for chicken sandwiches, too."

"Ah, Steve, you're too good to me. I hope your wife knows what a treasure she has."

"I think so. She's waiting in the car with the sleeping baby right now. Want to come out and say hi?"

"Sure. Come on outside and get your daily dose of vitamin D, darling," and picked up her daughter.

Steve held the door for her and waited for her response.

"You fixed it! No more Alaska winter modification. So that's why you wanted to borrow it."

"Well, I couldn't very well do it when you were using it every day. It took having a baby for you to take two days off work."

Mrs. Steve poked her head out of her window. "Let me see that baby. Good grief, she's a newborn and already bigger than mine. Now, I want you to take at least the rest of the week off. Alice is more than happy to field your calls. If she can't figure out where to get stuff while you're on maternity leave, I'll let her call you. Everybody's in a hurry in the summer, but all your good customers know about the baby. Shoot, I think half the calls are folks just wondering if you've had her yet. Now, get back inside. I only came out to drive our car. That little Sonic of yours is cute, but I think you're going to need an upgrade soon. But enough about that. I'm sure it'll all work out."

***

Months later - Christmas Eve

"Our first Christmas together. Well, I promise you that one of these days, you'll have a father. Or not. Depends on if the right man comes around. Or returns."

Kay tried not to be bitter, but even though Steve had been trying for four months, there was no trace of Jay. He had a beautiful daughter that he'd missed seeing turn over for the first time. If he didn't hurry up, he'd miss that first tooth and sitting up by herself, too. Did Jay even suspect he was a father?

No, she told herself for the kazillionth time; he thought he was sterile. He left town and there was no reason to look back. Yeah, right. What she thought was the beginning of a beautiful relationship, both business and personal, was just a 'get your feet and other parts' warm venture. A tumble in the sleeping bag. A 'I'll tickle your fancy if you tickle mine' fest.

"Stop it!" she said aloud. The baby startled and grasped the air, then went back to sleep.

"Quit making excuses for both of you," she whispered. "Steve said there was a contract out on him. He wasn't the type to scare easily, so there must have been something to it. Give him the benefit of the doubt now that you know a little something. Yeah, well, very little."

Knock, knock, knock.

Must be someone I know to be knocking so softly, she thought. "Just a minute," she said aloud as she put on her fleece robe.

"Hi."

Kay fainted.

Jay dropped the cat carrier and rushed forward to grab her before she hit the floor. He held her close, cuddling her like the long-lost love that she was, glad that she had passed out and he could have this moment to hold her, feel her, smell her, without having to explain why he had been AWOL for the last thirteen months.

He felt her shiver, and realized she was awake. "Can we

go inside?" he asked.

"Uh huh."

Jay let her get to her feet but held onto her shoulders. "Are you okay, or should I carry you in?"

Kay giggled at the suggestion, then realized that she wasn't dreaming and began working on a scowl. "What are you doing here?"

"Can we go inside and talk about it? It's warmer in there, even with this door open."

"Oh, shoot. Yeah, come in," she said, and rushed over to make sure the baby was out of the draft.

"There, there," she said, and patted her daughter's back until she settled back into a deep sleep.

"He's a lucky man and doesn't realize it," Jay said.

"Who is and what are you talking about?"

Jay set the carrier down by the front door and started to take off his boots, then realized he should ask first. "Can I stay a while? I think we have a lot to talk about."

"Yeah, and hell yeah. As in, 'Yeah, you can stay a while,' and 'Hell yeah, we have lots to talk about."

"The baby's father who ditched you. He was, or is, a lucky man, depending on whether you take him back or not. I guess doctors don't realize it and think they're something special. Was he good to you?"

"I still don't know what you're talking about. My doctor was a lady, and yes, she was very good to me."

"Your husband, the doctor who left you, was he good to you?"

"Jay, what have you been smoking? I have never been married to a doctor. Shoot, I haven't been married to anyone in ten years."

"So, you two weren't married. That's fine. Was he good to you and the baby?"

"Okay, I don't know where you're getting your information, or even why you're here, but I was never married or in a relationship with a doctor. Now my turn. Why are you here?"

"I heard you were married, so I backed out of your life. I heard you had his baby and then he got tired of you or found someone else—I heard it both ways—and that you were now on your own. I knew you never gave up your business, and I guess that's a good thing since the jerk probably won't pay child support…"

"Jay, for the umpteenth time, there has never been a

doctor in my life. *You're* the baby's father."

Jay collapsed into the seat he had been standing in front of. "No." He shook his head several times. "No. I can't be the father."

"Do you want a paternity test or would looking at her do? Everyone who knows you says she looks just like you."

"A girl? I guess I just thought you had a son. But I'm sterile. She has to be someone else's."

"We can have a test done on that, too, but you're the only man I have been with for three years. And the last guy I was with before you was Hawaiian. Sperm doesn't stay active in a woman's body for a year and a half, and this baby is definitely not Pacific Islander. So, surprise! You're a father."

As if on cue, the baby awoke, ready for her next meal. "Hey honey, guess who came to dinner? You're father. If he decides to stick around, maybe he'll grow up to be a daddy."

Kay held the baby up to Jay, letting her fuss until she was wide awake. "Looks just like you, dear."

Jay rubbed his hand over the top of her head and smiled. "She's gorgeous."

"Yeah, the one thing I couldn't figure out and neither

could the doctors: she doesn't have a soft spot, or at least much of one. Feel it, it's only about a half-inch across."

Jay gently felt the top of her head. "Well, I guess we don't need a paternity test. My mother said I was the same way. How much did she weigh?"

"A whopping nine and a half pounds."

Jay shrugged his shoulder and laughed softly. "I had her beat there. I came into this world at ten pounds on the nose. I don't think my mother ever forgave me for that."

"Here, I need to feed her or she'll get real loud in a hurry." Kay brought the baby close and sat down in the oversized recliner to nurse her.

"Kay, I am so sorry. Really, I had no idea. I guess you believe me that I thought you were married to someone else and that you had his child. I came back because word got back to me that you were alone again. And raising a child on your own. Shoot, I was ready to come back as soon as I heard you were single again, but to have a child, too? You needed someone to have your back." He looked around the spacious two-bedroom apartment. "But it looks like you're doing great by yourself," then sighed in frustration.

"I do okay," Kay said. "But go ahead with the rest of your

story."

"Anyhow, I saved every dollar I made except for a few I needed for replacing worn out boots and my missing winter coat, then I put a big down payment on a shop with an unfinished apartment above it. I was hoping you'd come to work with me. You wouldn't have to work basically out of your car, driving around, calling on customers with a baby, and I could repair stuff inside, not out in the cold or wet. Bush mechanicking non-stop for a year was okay, but I've had my fill of working outside. I don't think my toes will ever warm up."

"So, were you wanting to move in with me and that's why you brought your luggage? And are you using totes for suitcases now?"

"Well, I left my duffle bag with all my clothes and such at the front door. That's not a tote, though: that's kinda my apology gift. I really am sorry for not contacting you. I'll tell you all about it later, but right now…"

Meow, meow.

"You brought me a cat? Who is it? Kit Kringle?"

"Nope. I brought you *our* cat. Yardley, meet Kay, my wife if she'll have me."

Jay opened the carrier door and let the once feral cat come to him. He rubbed her neck behind her ears, hoping Kay had heard his soft proposal.

"Did you just ask me to marry you?"

Jay nodded, then offered her the cat to pet. "If you'll have us."

Kay patted her head with her free hand and grinned at her. "So, you're the female who's been keeping this guy away from me for all this time."

"No, she's not. She has been keeping me out of trouble, though. You two are the only females I've been near for just over thirteen months now."

"Well, get ready, mister, because there's one more coming into your life."

"What's her name?"

"Well, Jay, I sort of named her after me."

"Kay, Junior?"

"No, literally. As in, you're Jay, I'm Kay…"

Jay leaned over and kissed his daughter on the head. "Nice to meet you, Elle. Sorry I'm late, but I'll make it up to you and your mother. I promise."

** THE END **

Thank you!

I hope you enjoyed **Kit Kringle: An Alaskan Tale**. My characters have—or love—a challenge! Check these out:

The Fairies Saga

(historical fiction and/or time travel)

Naked in the Winter Wind

Ha'Penny Jenny

Aye, I am a Fairy

Dances Naked

Little Bear and the Ladies

Little Drummer Boy

Chasing Christmas

The Great Big Fairy

Never Too Young

Pool Boy Wanted: No Experience Preferred (spicy)

Luke the Unexpected

Time in a Little Blue Bottle

Arlie Undercover

Modern day action, suspense, romance about the Alaska detective with the smartest smartphone around!

A Stingray Christmas

The Biggest Heart Ever

Always a Bigger Fish (also has a Fairies Saga character or two crossing over!)

NEW (as of Summer 2018)

Contemporary romances

Be My Angel

Three Are One

One Arctic Summer

Contact information:

Web page: www.danihaviland.com

Email: dani@danihaviland.com

Twitter: @dani_haviland

Facebook: Dani Haviland Author

Book Bub: www.bookbub.com/authors/dani-haviland

Goodreads: http://bit.ly/2DHgdrds

www.ingramcontent.com/pod-product-compliance
Lightning Source LLC
Chambersburg PA
CBHW082013170626
46817CB00009B/3083